I0611680

He Ain't Dead Yet
Letters From A Woman Scorned

R. Nikki Chaney

He Ain't Dead Yet: Letters From A Woman Scorned

DEDICATION

This novel is dedicated to everyone that believed in me to include my mother, my boys, my sister and most importantly the love of my life, my husband. It is also dedicated to all survivors of domestic violence and abuse and most importantly to our "Fallen Queens." Your memory will forever live on. If you or anyone that you know is experiencing domestic violence and abuse, seek help immediately.

Heel My Heart, Corporation

404-824-3341

National Domestic Violence Hotline

800-799-SAFE (7233)

Anonymous and Confidential

ACKNOWLEDGMENTS

I would like to acknowledge Ken Chaney, Mr. Jeno of Creative Digital Photography, Tiffany Mosley of Confessions of Glamour and Tikira Ross for making this book cover spectacular.

.

June 1, 2004

Today started off as the best day of my life. I just found out that I'm going to be a mother. I've been holding it down with my boyfriend for 4 months now and we are about to be parents. Even though I'm only 19, I know that I'm going to be a great mother to (her.) My mom was the first one that I told. Her response was simple, "why in the hell are you so excited? He was just at the club last night with another woman all on his lap." How cold my exciting news bring such misery to my life? My dreams and unaccomplished goals will never be fulfilled. I was facing being a single mother. How could he? I've stood by his lies, drug dealing, and gang banging and promiscuous ways. He vowed that he would never cheat on me after the last time that I caught him. Should I even tell him about our child? I think not. Abortion it is.

Summer

January 19, 2007

Today is the worst day of my life. For the past year I've been cheating on my husband. Last week my sidepiece revealed to me that he was HIV positive and that I should go get tested. The room in my doctor's office caved in as he read my results. POSITIVE. All I could do was cry. This can't be. My fabulous life was about to end. How could I tell my husband that for the past year, not only have I been cheating, but to add insult to injury, that I may have infected him with the worst incurable virus on earth? I stood up, fixed my locking curls, reapplied my makeup and positioned myself to face the two men that I was in love with.

Mia

July 12, 2009

My head hung low and my heart raced with anticipation as I dialed the repeated number on my husband's cell phone bill. My hands were sweaty and my voice was shaky as a woman's voice came through the receiver. Speaking to this woman, my life flashed before me. The man that I had been with for 10 years, married to for 5, and birth 2 boys for was having an affair. I silently listened as this woman's words ripped my family apart. Upon hanging up the phone, all I could see was red. I wanted him dead. I had given him all of me. Sitting in the darkness viewing the shadows of what used to be a happy home; I planned my husband's murder.

Sharon

CHAPTER 1
PARIS

"Bryan, Sweetheart, we're moving absolutely too fast, don't you agree?" "Paris I want to be with you every day. I wouldn't feel right unless I woke up next to you every morning, Bryan said as he helped me unpack." My new home in Atlanta was absolutely gorgeous. I had finally closed the deal on a 4 bedroom, 3 ½ bathrooms, ranch-styled home. The upper level of my home consisted of a guest room, a full bath, and a bonus room that I decided to turn into a theater room. I sat back and watched as Bryan hung up some paintings on the wall. So much had been revealed about him since we started kicking it. Behind his handsome face, tattoos and dreads was a man that spent 3 years in prison on a drug conspiracy charge. Bryan happened to be the gentleman that was best friends to one of my best friends' son. That alone made me very skeptical of continuing a relationship with him. Despite my feelings, however, I couldn't resist and before he could even get his house arrest leg monitor off, he was moving in with me.

4

"Paris you never get tired of something that you love, Bryan said trying to continue justifying our arrangements." I rolled my eyes; thinking to myself that we had only been together a month and the "love" word was already being used. Sometimes you just got to ride the bike until the wheels fall off and that's exactly what I was used to doing. "You're right sweetheart. I got to trust that you are my dream come true, I said as I kissed him." The boys accepted Bryan, all except Jacarious, of course. "I just don't trust him, Mama. Why couldn't we just be in Atlanta alone, he would say?" Sometimes I really didn't know how to respond so it would always be the usual, "trust your mama on this, okay." I hated that my son felt this way but I wanted him to understand that I needed a special type of love and affection that I couldn't receive from them. Bryan was the youngest of 2 brothers and 1 sister. His parents were still together and had been married ever since his oldest brother was 6 months old. Bryan had 2 kids, a son named Bryan, Jr., who was 3 and a daughter named Harmony who was 5. Harmony and I bonded as soon as we met. I wasn't able to spend as much time with little Bryan, hell Bryan didn't even spend much time with little Bryan. As a matter of fact, he didn't even know him. When Bryan got busted and went to prison, Bryan, Jr.'s mother was pregnant with him so the relationship that was formed between Bryan and his son was soon developing after we had got together. Nonetheless the beginning of our relationship was definitely difficult. Bryan was on Federal Probation which prohibited him from leaving the state of Florida. Bryan totally ignored that clause under his probation. I met him in Valdosta, Georgia, so I knew that he didn't care about being in Atlanta without permission. He was working when I met him but of course by moving to Atlanta he was forced to quit. Bryan also had mandatory drug classes and drug testing every week. He would be in Florida more than he was here with me. On top of it all I had to provide a means for him to travel back and forth because without a job Bryan had no source of income. He wouldn't be able to get a job in Atlanta because of the obvious; he was not supposed to be here. Despite that all, Bryan and I had a serious connection. I know that it was our sexual chemistry that kept things steamy between us. It's extremely hard to find someone that you're sexually compatible with but when you do, hold on to that shit. For all the right reasons, Bryan had entered my world and I was excited about our new venture.

CHAPTER 2
SHARON

"Mama, why are you crying, asked Sharon's oldest son?"
Sharon couldn't hear a single word coming from her son's
mouth. She just sat there with a beeping phone in her hand,
eyes wide open, and her mind racing at an uncontrollable pace.
Sharon begins to chant, rocking back and forth, "he's cheating,
he's cheating," she said. Sharon picked up the phone to call
her husband of 5 years. It seemed as if years were passing by
before he finally answered. "Hello, a deep voice of aggravation
came through the receiver." "How could you Carter? I've
given you my whole life. How dare you? And your boys, why
would you do this to our family?" "I'm sorry, Carter said. I
never wanted to hurt you. This was all a mistake. Please
forgive me?" "Forgive you. Your asking for forgiveness
makes everything that this other woman had to say true then.
So it's true, a devastated Sharon, bawling as she was trying to
get her words out. It's true that you've been having an affair. I

7

don't know where you are but if I see you, you're dead, you hear me, DEAD, Sharon yelled as she slammed the phone down." Sharon continued to sit alone in the darkness of her home. She didn't even respond to her boys crying in the background. She battled telling her family. Sharon was from a small town in Georgia. She grew up in a home with her mother and younger sister. Sharon was always the strong one in her household. She defended her mom in her abusive relationships and protected her younger sister from what she considered to be the scum of the earth. Sharon's younger sister was wild. She always was interested in boys and living a fast life, where as Sharon, on the other hand, was more reserved. Growing up Sharon was blamed a lot for her singer sister's actions and endured lots of beatings whenever she interfered in her mother's affairs. As a child Sharon was very independent and determined to have a life greater than the one she lived and she vowed to never allow a man to her as they would do her mother. At the age 15 Sharon started working and establishing her independence. Sharon was a very stubborn child growing up and instead of chasing boys; she was more interested in getting away from the household that she viewed as "hell on earth." Right after high school graduation Sharon left for Job Corps and that would be the place where she would meet the man of her dreams. Carter Camon was one of the most outgoing and exciting guy on campus. Sharon didn't feel as if they had much in common but once they started dating it was discovered that they would have an everlasting love. Carter brought a sense of real love and stability that Sharon felt she never received at home. The way that he listened to her inner most deepest thoughts and comforted her when there wasn't anyone else around was what swept Sharon off her feet. Carter and Sharon had that "Oprah and Stedman" type of relationship on campus, so it wasn't farfetched that their relationship would flourish and blossom into an everlasting marriage. After college graduation, Sharon moved to Florida with Carter since that was where he was from. We all would like to think that every relationship has a Cinderella beginning and a Shrek ending but reality always reveal otherwise. Carter was no knight and shining armor; of course he had his prince charming ways but his other side consisted of chain smoking weed and small time hustling to make ends meet. It was hard for him to hold down a good job because of his daily habit and a pregnant Sharon realized that she had left a household of hell only to enter another one. Sharon loved Carter though and she stood by him until he attempted to mature. They were about to be parents so Sharon was certain that Carter would put away all of his childish ways. She worked and saved and by the time their second son was born, Sharon had saved enough money to purchase her first home. Things were finally looking up for Carter and Sharon. Carter was even blessed with a great job opportunity and even decreased his smoking habits. Hustling was also becoming obsolete. Are you existing or living? That was a question that Sharon no longer asked. She was living the dream life. After 6 years of being together, Carter had proposed and they finally got married. The worse part of getting married was shortly after Carter was arrested for violating his probation and was sentenced to 6 months in jail. This was very hard for Sharon to deal with but they toughed it out and when he was released everything was everything. It was back to the family outings, cruises, and dinner dates. Carter and Sharon had the perfect relationship, but now she sits here in dismay. What have I done wrong, Sharon wondered? Was it the mood swings, my child bearing weight or was it in fact that Carter just didn't love me anymore? A conclusion couldn't come to her head. What she did know was that Carter obviously was unhappy because this affair had been going on for months and that she needed to contact her Pastor immediately for spiritual guidance before she ended his life and hers.

CHAPTER 3
PARIS

Atlanta was such a great start for me and Bryan's relationship. Bryan worked diligently on getting his probation transferred to Georgia as we worked on building a foundation that could not crumble. Everyone was adapting. The boys loved their school which was 5 minutes up the street and they were all managing well despite the recent suicide of my husband. All of my family was shocked to discover that I had moved on so quickly. I was even shocked. Truthfully I wasn't ready to move on but the Pisces in me always placed others feelings before my own. Right before I moved here, I had a conversation with Bryan about my feelings toward living with someone and that I honestly wasn't ready to share my space with anyone and he cried his poor heart out. I have a weakness for a man in tears; it sincerely does something to me. It's no way that I could just leave him there crying that way so I placed my feelings aside for the well being of his. During the day things would go great for me but it was at night that I would feel a sense of displacement. My marriage and the way that it ended were constantly racing through my mind. My husband always wanted the best for me and he always would tell me that a man should always provide for me and the boys and never put our life in jeopardy and that he should place me on a pedestal because a woman of my stature deserves that. Bryan wasn't doing any of these things but a part of me knew that once he was stable that he would but I certainly was growing impatient taking care of him. Taking care of him was definitely not a part of the plan and it was taking a toll on me. One early morning after dropping the boys off, I stared at him and just couldn't take it anymore. "Bryan, I yelled and pushed him as he slept soundly without a care in the world." "Whaatt, he yelled from under the covers." "Wake up. We need to talk." "About what baby? Dang, I'm trying to sleep." "Exactly. That's the issue right there, you sleeping. You need to wake your ass up and go do something productive. If I had known it would be this difficult for me by being with you, I would've left your ass in Florida." I guess that statement struck a nerve because that nigga jumped up like he was about to do something. "Paris yo ass tripping. It's too early for this shit, damn. If you weren't so confused in your own life maybe you could see a real nigga in front of you." "What in the hell do you mean, confused in my own life? Look Bryan, I'm not trying to argue sweetie but it's okay for me to lay around all day but a man is suppose to take care of his family and you are not fulfilling your God-given obligations." "Paris what am I supposed to do when I'm not even suppose to be up here?" "I sure can tell you what you shouldn't be doing. You shouldn't be hanging out all night and coming in all kinds of hours, spending my money like crazy, or driving all my gas out without putting more in. It's only been three months since we have been here and we're already having arguments. I've had plenty restless nights and more empty bank accounts than one could imagine." Bryan didn't respond so I left out the room to go cook breakfast. When I returned he was sleep again. I was so angry looking at him. Like really, nothing that I just said even mattered. It was men like this that my mom warned me about and that my husband said I was too good for. Bryan was one to always hit you with "a real woman would stay by her man while he's down." I soon realized that that slogan only applied to married couples not niggas that are down and out when you meet them. A real man wouldn't pursue a woman with kids; knowingly he couldn't even provide a living for himself. Those are definitely the men that you say thanks, but no thanks to. Damn it's too late for me. I already love him.

CHAPTER 4
PARIS

Four months had passed and the only thing that secured my attachment to Bryan was our sexual chemistry. I stood and watched Bryan as he mowed the yard one day. There were some good qualities in Bryan. I mean he could cook his ass off and he would maintain the yard and would even do laundry and the dishes from time to time but I believed that he was so willing to do things for monetary items in return. I was sitting on the edge of my king size bed, playing with a stuffed animal that Jacarious had won for me at the fair, when Bryan, sweaty from head to toe, entered the bedroom. "Hey, babe can we talk?" "I know you want to talk babe but can you please give me time to shower and I promise I'll be all yours, he said kissing me on my forehead." I rolled my eyes and took a deep sigh as I left the room. My back patio was the most relaxing, especially with a fresh cut lawn, so I sat there gathering my thoughts until Bryan was done. Looking over my life, it wasn't one relationship that I could remember that I was truly happy in. I gave eight long years to the father of my kids and the best thing to come out of that were my precious little boys. Then, I met whom I thought to be the husband of my dreams and that turned out to be a nightmare. However, with everything in life you should always look for the lesson. My husband taught me self-worth. I am a woman of value, prestige, and honor and I'll be damned if I allow anyone to treat me any less than royalty. I deserve the best because God says so. Once I muscled up the strength to tell Bryan how I felt, I came back in the house. When I walked in the room, Bryan was dropping his towel. His tall and tatted body was even sexier wet. He motioned me to come here as he tied his dreads back. Bryan grabbed me into his arms and started kissing my neck as he grabbed a handful of my butt. I already knew what was about to go down. Bryan laid me down on the bed, slid my shorts off, placed one of my legs over his shoulder as he began to massage my breasts and made my body explode with his tongue. After his tantalizing tongue performance, he flipped me over and began pounding me from the back. He always lifted one leg on the bed as he pleased me from behind so that he could enter further. I was in heaven and totally disregarded all of Bryan's flaws in that moment. Midday sex was always the best. I awoke before Bryan, as usual, and all of my previous thoughts invaded my mind. Sex with Bryan was always a distraction but it never failed, as soon as it was all said and done, my true feelings would emerge. I took a deep sigh and tugged at Bryan. "Babe we need to talk. My mind has been made up for a while now and I've come to the conclusion that I'm not totally happy with our relationship." "What, Bryan said interrupting?" "No let me finish. All you do is take, take, take and frankly I'm tired of providing for you and your kids when you can't do anything for me and mine. Don't get me wrong, I knew exactly what I was getting myself into but I never expected things to get this bad. I think it's best for you to go back home until your probation is transferred. That's the best way for us to work things out, because at least you would be able to get a job." I guess Bryan was fed up as well, because before I could finish, he had jumped up and started packing. I stood back and watched him pack without saying a word. I was torn between my heart and my mind and that was confusion and God is not the Author of confusion. My heart was saying "don't leave," but my mind was saying "get the hell out." "Paris you're right, Bryan began as he kept packing. I have been living off of you and that's not something that I'm accustoming to doing. I'm accustoming to providing for my woman and giving her all that life has to offer, but I just can't do that for you right now." He continued packing the remaining of his things, including his studio equipment. I guess through all of the turmoil I forgot to mention that Bryan was also a talented rap artist, unsigned that is. He looked at me after he had everything packed, kissed me on the cheek and left. I stood in the room and stared out the window as he drove away.

CHAPTER 5
SHARON

Sharon was battling suicide every day. Her husband's affair had really taken over her life, the life that she had worked so hard to achieve. Even though she still went to work, her mind was so spaced out that she couldn't even remember how she got there, what she accomplished, or when she left. One Sunday during church service when her Pastor opened up the doors for prayer Sharon rose from her seat and proceeded down front. Her Pastor made a cross on her head with oil and began to pray a miracle over her life. Sharon felt a burden lift up from her shoulders as she began to weep. Her body felt a rush of uncontrollable emotions but Sharon was feeling the Holy Ghost Spirit and she never felt better in her life than in that moment. After service Sharon's boys played around while she had a heart to heart with her Pastor and his wife. "Pastor, I remember the times when we were at our best. I remember the trips and the holidays, but most of all I remember when we started coming to church and praising God together as a family. What happened to us? What happened to me?" The Pastor's wife grabbed Sharon's hand. "Sharon in Life not all things are meant to last. God brings along temporary things in order to bless us with what He wants to be everlasting. You have two little boys that you are raising to be great and you should recognize the power of God. I'm not saying that you never had a relationship with God but this is a test of faith. God will never take you to anything that He wouldn't pull you through. You're strong Sharon and this test will soon be you your testimony." Their conversation that was merely an hour provided Sharon with information that would last a lifetime. Before Sharon was getting ready to leave, her pastor offered her a job within the church. He wanted Sharon to orchestrate different church events. Sharon's job was to plan, organize, and create a musical Holy Fest for the church. She got all the details so that she could get stared expeditiously. Sharon was extremely excited about the project. It had been six months since Carter's infidelity ripped their marriage in half and today was the first day that Sharon felt great. As Sharon prepared dinner she jotted down ideas for the event. She had come up with a design for the flyer but was battling with a name. Sharon decided to call her sister for some inspiration. It had been a minute since they had spoken. Sharon didn't want her voice to give off any signals of dismay so she avoided talking to her mom and her sister as often as possible. "Hellur, a squeaky and country tone answered." "What's up chic?" "Nothing much, just being fabulous, Sharon's sister Paris answered." "Look, I'm planning a church event. I'm inviting different praise dancers from various churches across Pensacola to dance. We will be having food and lots of entertainment for the kids. I've come up with a great design for the flyer but I'm stuck on a name for the event." "Okay, so you say it's going to be dancing and food and you didn't invite me, dismissed boo, Paris said laughing. No, but a good name for that event would be "Praise Jump-off." "I love that,

Sharon said." "So how are you doing Sharon? How are my nephews? I haven't heard from you all in a minute." "Everything is cool girl. I've just been working and helping out with the church. The boys have so much going on with sports and all, I be ready to knock out as soon as I hit the door. Some of us do have jobs Paris." "Girl I work. I'm letting these bum ass niggas work my nerves that is. I had to send Bryan packing girl. I don't know why I pick these guys that I have to save." "I don't either child. You should have just moved to Atlanta alone. You rush relationships. Sit back sometimes and just enjoy your blessings and your boys for once. Get to know Paris." Sighing, "I know. Hopefully this separation will work. Where's Carter?" "Girl I gotta go. My food is burning." Sharon quickly hung up the phone to avoid a conversation about Carter. Sharon continued cooking as she contemplated on calling her sister back. She really hated holding all of this in. As soon as she picked up the phone to dial Paris back, a call came through. Sharon heart dropped. She hadn't heard this ringtone in six months. She looked at the phone with rage wondering if she should answer or not. "Hello, Sharon said in an angry voice." "Sharon please talk to me. I can't go on like this. I've fell off like a pair of baggy pants. I'm smoking weed more than I ever had before and I've even tried something much harder to cope with the pain. "That's nothing new Carter, Sharon interrupted Carter's plea for forgiveness." "I know how I used to smoke but now I'm smoking 9-10 blunts a day, laced blunts. I can't live without you and I know that my boys miss me. How could you tear our family apart?" "Me. How could I tear our family apart? You did this. You; and don't act as if the boys are your concern. You could care less about being a father. Furthermore, it's your indiscretions that I can't forgive or forget. Goodbye. This conversation is over." Sharon hung up the phone. He has some never calling me. Talking about the boys miss him. I bet he hasn't lost any weight or any sleep since all of this surfaced. All of these lies. I'm not one to fall for it though. He played me and now it's time for payback.

CHAPTER 6
PARIS

Two months had passed since Bryan had left and even though we talked every day something was still missing. Bryan was even starting to give off signs that he was cheating. Most of the times when I called he was always available but now he was always in the studio. He spent all of his time perfecting a hobby while I made a financial living for him. It puzzled me that he wouldn't at least get a part-time job while he was there. My sister was right. I wished that I would have just concentrated on me and the boys. I had my own kids to provide for. A guy calling himself a man should be able to take care of himself, not look to a woman for it. This was such a distraction and the holidays were right around the corner.

Another Friday night and I was stuck in the house bored and lonely. I decided to call my sitter and escape for a little while. Atlanta nightlife had so much to offer. I cruised around the city until I ran up on one of my favorite night spots. In my state of mind, this was really the last place that I should've ended up, but what the hell, I thought. I stepped out, dressed in all black and smiled at the gorgeous valet as I strutted into Trapeze. This was the ultimate getaway but you definitely have to be real open minded to enjoy a spot of this caliber. Eye candy was everywhere in the V.I.P. I was an exclusive member long before I moved to Atlanta, even though Bryan didn't know, however this was my first time coming alone. Before I moved up here, I used to frequent Trapeze with one of Atlanta's finest club owners. This guy had a well known name to all and to keep our business on the low this was our secret location. It was kind of weird without him here with me but I made my way back to the clothing free area or "play house" as we called it. That was our favorite location as we were able to be as private or voyeuristic as we pleased. Tonight it was plenty to do and plenty to see. As I sat and watched a couple's performance, someone walked up behind me saying, "we always put on a show better than that." I turned around and there he stood. "Paris. Paris. Sneaking into town, I see." "Sneaking. Maybe you should check your messages on the disconnected number that I have, I said as I began to walk away." "Wait a minute baby. Things were getting to heated. Work was getting in the way and yes I was a little pissed to her that you had gotten married. Anything to say about that? Damn Shawty." "Shawty. Okay. Whatever. Um, let me see. Well I got married. This man tried to kill me and my boys but ended up killing himself. I moved to Atlanta, but not before getting involved with a bum ass nigga that I've been with for about five months now. How's your life, I asked with sarcasm?" "Damn baby. I'm sorry. He tried to do what. Come here baby. I'm so, so sorry. I can't believe that you went through all of this, he said as he consoled me, holding me tightly." I forgot how good he used to smell as I inhaled the Tom Ford cologne seeping through his Akoo cardigan. We caught up for awhile as we walked around enjoying the view. It was just like old times. "Hey, it was great seeing you, but I really have to run, I said before things between us got a little more physical." "What's the rush? At least let me walk you out." We exchanged numbers while the valet went for the car. "Paris, come on. Let's not end the night like this baby. We live in the same area. Leave your car and I'll take you home. You know you hate driving." I really did hate driving, so I took him up on his offer. "Wait. Let's take my car, I said. Your driver can come get you. I don't want to leave my car out here." I hated getting into situations that I knew I couldn't handle. This man was so wrong for me and I knew it. He had a woman, a wife to be exact but we had been carrying on for two years on and off since we met and he was not the type of guy that a normal girl like me could just walk away from. Once we arrived, I released my sitter, but before I had the chance to pay her, he pulled out $200 and told her thank you. My sitter stood there for a moment in complete awe. It wasn't because of the money though. I just smiled at her and put one finger over my mouth. I showed him to my bedroom as I went to kiss the boys good night. I was tired and a little tipsy so I undressed and lay down without even showering. He stared at me as I stared at him. "So you got big thangs popping, huh, he said grabbing me on top of him?" "Funny. Cute analogy though, I said trying to break away." Before I knew it though, he was kissing me and my body just couldn't resist. We made love all into the night and Bryan didn't even cross my mind. I slept well into the night on a man's chest that didn't even belong to me. Awaken by the early morning's sun, all I could hear was the lyrics to that song "As We Lay." This man was so fine, talented, business savvy, and so into me, but I couldn't help but think that when he left here he was going home to her. It was also amazing that he never wanted me with anyone. He constantly told me not to give his cookie away and what he would do if I did. I used to think that he just loved me so much and couldn't stand the fact that I was with any other man outside of him but in actuality that was his form of control. He never really loved me. He just loved the time that we shared and loved having control over me. We as women can be so manipulated by men sometimes. I tried to pull away from him slowly to not wake him. I went in the bathroom to brush my teeth and shower. I listened to Yolanda Adams station on Pandora as the steam from the shower relaxed my entire body. I closed my eyes and bent over to rest my head on the side of the shower and allowed the water to run down my back. Images of Jorese, William, and Bryan flashed through my head. All of these guys were so different, yet so similar. Different in age, background and appearance but similar in treating me like a peasant. They all treated me less than a queen. William I praised because he was the one that presented perfection when in actuality he was a devil in disguise. People, just like milk and food, have an expiration date. I wanted William to be perfect and I hid all of his flaws from others probably better than he did, but through time, I begin to despise him. The devil used William to try and take me out. Rather it was me or any other woman; his time had expired here on earth. I wanted everyone to think that I had finally chosen a man that loved me instead of me once again choosing wrong. I stayed in a marriage pretending all was well just to make the world think that I was on top. I didn't love myself. How could I stand by someone that not only try to kill me but my boys? They are my world and I thank God that He protected them, because no mother in the world could imagine how it feels to watch as someone tries to take away the most precious gift that God can give; their children. I started thinking that something was wrong with me. All of the men that I settled with abused me some type of way. I got out of the shower and stared reality in the face. I was the problem. A man won't do any more than a woman allows him to do. I walked out the bathroom and looked at another failure in my life. This man was never going to leave his wife for me. I was merely a tipoff. After this encounter with him, I vowed to myself that I would never get involved with him again.

CHAPTER 7
PARIS

Bryan and I was involved again for a couple days now and I
was back on track, despite my little rendezvous. Bryan had
decided to visit for the weekend. I said it was cool and it had
been about three weeks since "the other man" and I had even
spoke. This reaction I knew all so well. What is the need for
communication? He saw me. He got what he wanted. He
disappeared. I knew why I got into a relationship with him and
I also knew exactly why it would never go anywhere. You will
never experience happiness bringing misery to someone else's
life. His wife may have not known about me but I knew about
her and that alone made it wrong. I was content with his
decision, because the day that he left, I had a made up mind
about our relationship. I had my own man and he was on his
way to see me. I was waiting with anticipation as Bryan said
that he had a surprise for me. I cleaned up a little and ordered
pizza. It was a Friday night and he would be arriving late, so I

figured pizza was the best option. Bryan called before he got to our exit, so I added the last finishing touches to my face, slipped on a sexy black negligee and a pair of sexy pumps. I walked to the door when I heard his car pull up. I stood in the door looking sexy waiting to see his reaction when he bent the corner. His mouth dropped when he saw me and that was exactly the reaction that I was looking for. "Looks like I was missed, he said grabbing a handful of my ass." I led him into the house. I had lit candles all through the house and the bedroom was filled with a lavender aroma. The look on Bryan's face didn't change as I led him into the bathroom. The bathroom was also lit up like a 4th of July night. The Jacuzzi was filled with sliced apples and a bowl full of sliced apples sat on the side. A chilled bottle of Rose' sat in the wine bucket on the small table that was decorated for two. I slowly began to remove Bryan's clothes as Chris Brown's "Wet the Bed" played in the background. I knew my take charge role wouldn't last long. Bryan was the type of man that had to be in control and that's what I loved about him. He grabbed my hands and held them over my head as he lick me up and down, peeling my Vickie's off with his teeth. Once our bodies were completely naked, Bryan scooped me up and sat me in the tub. "Baby I missed you so much, Bryan moaned as he continued to kiss me all over. Didn't you miss me?" "Well of course, I said motioning my hand around at our set up." We continued to engage in each other for hours or shall I say until our fingers and toes began to wrinkle.

CHAPTER 8
SHARON

"Good afternoon everyone, said the well dressed, tall, beautiful woman standing in front of the class. I'm Susan Marshall and I will be directing your next path. As we all know all of us have experienced a certain loss and we are all here to help heal each others' heart." Finally, after several attempts Sharon was finally convinced by her pastor to attend a woman's group. Sharon is very protective of her feelings and was very reluctant as this program encouraged all individuals to share their deepest most intimate thoughts and feelings. Looking around the room as the beautiful woman continued to speak Sharon noticed all types of women, women of different ages, ethnicity and appearance. Really, what am I doing here Sharon questioned as she continued to listen and scan the room? Am I really ready to share with these women the pain and the hurt that Carter caused me? Sharon's thoughts were quickly interrupted. "Excuse me. We're all introducing ourselves. What is your name, asked by the beautiful woman teaching the class?" Sharon clears her throat again, Sharon, Sharon Camon is my name." "Hi Sharon said the array of women." After everyone spoke Sharon confidently stood and said "I don't think this class is for me," and proceeded to walk out. "Excuse me for just a second said the beautiful woman as she proceeded to follow me out the door. Sharon, Sharon waiter said the beautiful woman let me talk to you for just a moment. I know that this class may seem a little out of place and you may feel like you can't trust any of us with your most intimate feelings, but I assure you Sharon that we are all here and we are all in this together. Please, please allow this class to heal your heart." The beautiful woman then grabbed Sharon's hand gently touched her face and asked Sharon to please stay. Sharon looked away as she heard the small chatter coming from inside the walls of where she would now be sharing the pain and the hurt that Carter caused her. "Miss Marshall I must admit that my husband caused me a lot of pain and I'm still dealing with a lot of hurt but I thank you for stopping me from leaving. I promise you that I will make the best of this." The beautiful woman looked at Sharon and Sharon look back at her looking into her beautiful brown eyes, which displayed concern and sincerity as she was led back into the class. Once back in the class Sharon decided to sit in the back as to not disturb the others that were still carrying on their small conversations. Miss Marshall took her stance in front the class as she proceeded to give more information about the program and about the foundation Heel My Heart; H.E.E.L. Sharon wondered why it was called Heel My Heart, H.E.E.L. instead of Heal My Heart, H.E.A.L. She would soon find out. Miss Marshall spoke for about 30 more minutes, which felt like an hour yet I held on until the end when she decided to divide us all up into small groups. Even though I wasn't thrilled about the small groups I stayed despite and actually met a real good friend. "Hi, I'm Mia said the beautiful woman as she extended her hand out to me." Shaking Mia's hand, I was astounded by her beauty. Mia had to be about 5"5 with beautiful, long and curly hair pulled back in a pony tail. She wore a high waist tight fitting skirt a beautiful blouse and a nice pair of 5 inch Christian Louboutin heels. I couldn't help but notice her perfect posture and how her legs crossed beautifully. "Hi Mia. I'm Sharon and it's very nice to meet you." "So how do you feel Sharon you know with this class and all, Mia asked?" "Well, I guess it's okay I'm not too thrilled about sharing my feelings with a group of women that I don't know, but hey, I guess I need to start somewhere." "That's exactly how I feel, Mia said." An awkward silence felled between Mia and I as we scan the room to see what the other women were discussing. "Attention everyone, Miss Marshall announced from the front of the room. I just wanted to advise you guys that the group that you all were assigned was based on the evaluation forms that you filled out before entering the program. All of you are experiencing somewhat of the same situations. These situations have determined who to partner you with based on the comfort that each of you can provide the other individual. Hopefully this information will allow you all to openly discuss your situation with each other. We have about 15 more minutes and then we will conclude this meeting for today and I will see you all again next Wednesday, 3 PM." I really didn't want to discuss my situation first. I looked at Mia hoping that she will be more open than I was. Of course she was. I noticed that Mia was very chatty and eager to talk once she felt comfortable with me. I did wonder though, before she started to speak, what situation could we possibly have in common. Mia didn't look as if she belonged here. She didn't have eyes filled with pain. I was curious and a little anxious at the same time. As Mia began to speak I gave her my undivided attention. She began by stating that she had no kids. She really didn't have to say it. Looking at her figure I knew it. "Well Sharon, as I said, I don't have any kids and I was married for 5 years to a wonderful man." My eyes rose with suspicion. If she was married to a wonderful man, what was she doing in this class? I continued to listen. "For the past 3 years I have been having an affair with another man." When Mia made that statement I paused and gasped for air. Here it was, I am a very good woman and a very good wife and I'm cheated on but yet little Miss prissy, little Miss beautiful here has this wonderful husband that she cheats on. I began to feel anger rise as I continued to listen to Mia. "Don't get me wrong Sharon, I really did love my husband, Mia said. It's just that he was too consumed with his job and have been for the past 3 years. We hardly spent any time together and he forgot our anniversary every year. I met this guy one night when I went out and he just charmed me, wined and dined me made me feel like a woman again. I gave Mia a look of disgust and before I had a chance to tell her ass off, Miss Marshall said that the time was up for today. I thought good for little Miss prissy because I was about to go in on that ass. "Well ladies, I hope that you all were able to cover some common ground today and I hope that all of you will be returning back next Wednesday. If you need to get in touch with me, you all have my cards you can call me or you can email me and I will be sure to get back with you as soon as possible. I wish you all a great day and I look forward to seeing you on next week." When Miss Marshall concluded her speech, I grabbed my exclusive Prada Bag that Carter purchased for me on my birthday last year and proceeded to exit the building before Little Miss prissy could say anything else to damage our potential friendship. Before I could escape quietly Mia came running. "Sharon, Sharon wait. I wanted to know if we could exchange numbers and maybe have coffee sometime. I was a little reluctant because Mia got on my damn nerves with her story, but I figured maybe she could revive herself after a few talks with me. I despise a cheating woman and even more I despise a cheating woman that cheats on a good man. Although I didn't know Mia's husband the mere fact that she said he was wonderful I knew that he was way too much for her. I grabbed one of my business cards out of my bag and handed one to Mia as she done the same. I noticed that Mia was carrying an exclusive Gucci Soho bag, one that I always wanted. Mia obviously was well-off and I wondered what did her husband do? Was he really selfish and did he really drive her into the arms of another man? Coffee sounded nice, but I figured Little Miss Mia would easily spill the beans if she had a couple of Cosmos. "Thank you, I said as Mia handed me her card." Before I could walk away, Mia yelled, "Sharon, I just wanted to tell you that you are very beautiful and whatever any man done to you it was his loss." I was shocked to hear her say this. Even though I didn't talk about my situation she was still able to see the goodness in me without me saying a word. Maybe Mia and I could be friends after all, I thought as I smiled at her and walked away. Walking alongside the busy sidewalk, I noticed the sign for the class that I had left. It was beautiful. Two high heels with hearts extending from the ends of them. Original, I thought as I continued to my car. I drove a nice BMW 745. Carter had purchased it for me for our anniversary two years ago and I loved it. As I was backing out of the parking lot, I noticed Mia standing by her car talking on her cell phone. Mia drove a Mercedes S550 black with tinted windows. I knew Mia had to have a nice car with the way she was dressed and all. I waved at Mia as I backed out and put in my new Yolanda Adams CD. I need this praise break as I cruised down the streets of Pensacola Florida.

CHAPTER 9
MIA

I waved goodbye to Sharon as I sat in the parking lot and argued with Chase. Chase had been my boo for the past three years now. Chase and I have been through so much and even though he didn't want me my body still wanted him. "Look Mia, there's nothing else that we have to discuss, please just leave me alone." I felt tears begin to form in my eyes as chase constantly killed my pride. My divorce was finally final and I couldn't fathom why Chase hadn't come to his senses. Look at me. I'm hella sexy, very professional and very established, what man wouldn't want me? "Chase stop saying this. I love you. You love me. We should be together. Hello, hello, I said before noticing that Chase had hung up the phone. Fuck you I yelled to the dial tone." I jumped in my car and sunk down in the seat as I cried uncontrollably. Chase was confused. How could he do this to me? I gave him my all and in a quick second he destroyed my life. I wiped my tears, got my composure and reapplied my makeup. I'm Mia, Mia Lancer, formally Bradford, Florida's Finest. Get with me or get ran the fuck over. Me run behind a man, never. I'm done. Adjusting my mirror, I strapped on my seatbelt, put in that new BSG mixtape and sped off. "Are you ok Chase, his friend asked as he sat with his phone to his ear? "Yeah, I'm cool." "Did she break down again?" "What do you think?" "Look, don't snap on me. I'm just being concerned." "I'm sorry, Chase said to his friend. It's just that I know I did Mia wrong. I led her on and even after I gave her the worst news ever, she still finds it in her heart to love me." "It will be ok. Come here and let me make it all better." Chase placed his phone down and entered the arms of his lover, his man, Derek.

While cruising down Davis Highway, I thought about my life and how much it had changed. It really hadn't taken a turn for the worse if only Chase would be with me. I thought about Blake and how much of a good man he was to me. Blake would do anything in the world for me, how could I betray him the way that I did? He never deserved it just as I feel I don't deserve what Chase is doing to me, but, where I'm from Karmas last name was Bitch. Blake was an educated ex street hustler. He was 6"1, light skinned and built. He had a body straight out of a magazine. His dreads were always neatly twisted and edged up nicely with his goatee which he kept trimmed to perfection twice a week. I met Blake back in 2001. I frequent a bar called Coconuts and that particular night I was dressed to impress. I wore a long sleeve black XO Collection dress that hugged my every curve, v-cut in the front nicely so that you could see the sides and roundness of my perky breasts. The back was low cut just revealing enough to make your imagination want to see more and I topped it off with a pair of black Tom Ford heels. I was at the bar when Blake approached me. "Hello pretty lady. Is this seat taken, he asked in his best Morris Chestnut voice?" I turned around to face him, purposely crossing my legs to get his attention and said, "why yes it is." "Excuse me. You appeared to be alone." "Well, I was until this handsome, irresistible man asked me "is this seat taken". He smiled and sat down beside me. "Thanks for the invite, he said." Blake and I got to know each other while the music played and the drinks kept flowing. I told him that I was an attorney for a private firm and he told me that he was an ex hustler who had started his own construction company, well companies. Blake owned 3 of the biggest construction companies in the state of Florida. I was indeed impressed. He was single, received his Masters Degree in Business, had his own company, no kids and may I add, fine as hell. It seemed as if we had known each other for a lifetime. He had been single for 2 years and I had been single for one. Even though I had one cut buddy during that year, nothing became serious and my body hadn't been sexually healed in 5 months. I stared at Blake as he licked his lips and removed the hair from my face. His touch made my body shiver. God I wanted this man. Who was I kidding? I needed this man. Everything about him was perfect. He could definitely make me a wife. I've never considered being married before, but damn this man was perfect. Blake and I danced a little and talked until the lights came on. I was waiting to see any imperfections when the lights came on but this man didn't possess any. He looked better. He wore a tan blazer, Michael Kors, white button down and a pair of Tru Religion jeans, topped off with some suede Salvatore Ferragamo loafers. His wrist sparkled with a Gucci timeless stainless steel watch. "Can't believe the night is over, Blake said." "Yeah, I know right, I said." Hoping that he would say let's make this night last forever, but Blake was a gentleman. He walked me out to my car, gave me a kiss on the cheek and popped my business card saying this number will change his life. I knew that he would call because he wanted me just as bad as I wanted him. I watched him as he walked away. Blake drove a brand new

Mercedes G Wagon, black with chrome. Everything about this man drove me crazy. I fixed my hair and makeup in the mirror and just when I was about to pull off, Blake called. "Hello, I said." "Hey Mia, I was wondering what your morning was looking like?" "Well, I plan on attending Worship Service." "Can I attend the Worship Service?" I could barely contain my composure; to top it all off, Blake was a Godly man. This indeed is my husband. Two years later, my dream came true. I was Mrs. Blake Bradford. The honking horn behind me broke my daydreaming. The only blessing out of this affair is that I didn't ruin my husband's life due to my infidelity.

CHAPTER 10
PARIS

I laid in a daze as I stared at the engagement ring that Bryan had placed on my finger. Twirling it round and round, thinking of how much I wanted to leave him and he comes back with a diamond ring, wanting me to be Mrs. Bryan Smith. After Bryan and I bathed, he sent me on a miniature scavenger hunt. Look here; look there, until I found the note that said, "now come back to the one who loves you." It was so romantic. I thought that I would cry when he proposed, but I actually felt numb. Guess I wasn't expecting that or maybe it was because of my little sexual escapade. I thought about telling Bryan but I didn't want to ruin the moment so I just admired the ring in the shining moonlight through the bedroom window. Due to Bryan's work schedule, he could only stay the weekend. I hated to see him leave Sunday, but I knew he had to go. My night couldn't have been any better and I never thought that it would start off anything less than how it ended. I got up to cook breakfast before Bryan left. "Good morning baby. You got it smelling right up in here, he said as he kissed me from behind." "Morning love. How was your night?" "Really, you don't remember all this, Bryan said, poking me with his weapon of destruction." I finished cooking breakfast while Bryan and the boys got the trash together to take out. "Make sure you guys wash your hands, breakfast is about ready, I yelled." I made sure to add extra love while fixing Brian's plate this morning. Steak, eggs, grits, toast and a bowl of fruit was all decorated to perfection. I prepared the boys plates and sashayed to the bedroom. Walking in my 4" pumps to my bedroom, looking good, I closed the door and locked it behind me, removed my bathrobe and revealed underneath something very sexy for my man to see. I walked over to the side of the bed to serve my man as he was well deserving of it, but before I could sit his plate down, Bryan held up a club wrist band. "What's this Paris?" I was shocked. "What do you mean Bryan? I don't know what that is?" "Don't play me with that bullshit. I found it in the trash can taking out the trash. Now who the fuck been over here?" "I don't know where you got that from but no one has been over here Bryan." "This wristband belongs to a man. It's too big for your arm, so where the fuck were you or who was over here?" Slamming his plate down on the table and feeling guilty as hell, I said "I don't know what you're talking about and I stormed out the bedroom." Bryan didn't say anything as this was his typical way of responding to things when he knew I was lying. He finished eating his breakfast without saying anything to me, packed up his things and left. I wanted to stop him. I wanted to say something, but shit I was guilty and I didn't want to say anything else to incriminate myself. I watched out the window as Bryan drove away blasting his new CD. I figured I would call him once he was about two hours away. Well, well, this bitch wants to play me, Bryan said. Glad I got my back up plan. I pulled up slowly to the Blockbuster up the street from where Paris and I lived, wondering if I could catch Amy at work. Amy was the chic that I met at Blockbuster one night picking up a movie for Paris and I to watch. She was a bad bitch. Tall, dark skin and down for a nigga. We exchanged numbers that night, but we just been texting every now and then, mostly when I got mad at Paris. It was time for us to get a little physical now that I know Paris is playing me. I walked in and to my surprise, she was there looking good as hell. "What's up stranger, I said, watching her voluptuous ass as she bent over getting all the returned movies from the bin." "Well, hi stranger, she said. What brings you into my neck of the woods today? Coming to get another flick for you and your wifey to watch, she said, laughing." "Matter of fact I was coming to see if you could take a little break." "I was actually about to take one. Give me about five minutes." I walked back outside to smoke a cigarette. My nerves were bad and I didn't know what I was about to do, but if something happened it must was meant to happen. I sat in the car watching as Amy grabbed her stuff. She was so damn sexy walking out to the car. "So what do you have in mind Bryan?" I was just hoping that we could talk get to know each other a little better I know that we've been texting for the last month or so. Just feel like it's time for you to get to know a nigga, you know on a more physical level. "Physical, soooo you and your wife are not together anymore, I'm assuming." "First off, she's not my wife and second off, no, I, mean we straight but I really don't feel like talking about her. What's up with me and you?" "You know I've really been feeling you and I was hoping this day would come soon, Amy said as she started to take her jacket off. Obviously she's not pleasing you so let me give you something to remember." Before I could say anything Amy had unzipped my pants, pulled out my throbbing knob and begin to blow it. Shit, I moaned as she sucked and sucked and sucked. This girls head game was definitely something not to be reckoned with. She continued to suck and lick looking up into my eyes every now and then and before I could stop it I exploded all in her mouth. Oh my God, and she swallowed it licking every bit of my juices. We both sat in silence for a while. I couldn't believe what I had just done. I mean, I really don't know what Paris did, maybe I overreacted, but it was nothing that I could do to change what just happened between Amy and me. "You're very quiet. I mean, did I not do a good job or something?" "Don't feel that way baby. Everything is good on your end, it's just that I hate that happened and now I got to leave." "Oh, you were on your way back home?" "Yeah I got to get back to the house. My probation will be transferred next week, though, so we can spend plenty of time together again." "I mean, why are you coming back if you guys are not together anymore?" "Look, I never said that Paris and I weren't together anymore, I just said for you not to worry about it, Bryan snapped." "Look, I got to be going so hit me up alright." Amy leaned over and gave me a kiss on the cheek put her jacket on and got out of the car. I sat there for a moment thinking about her thinking about Paris, thinking about how I was about to juggle these two women that live minutes apart. Fuck it, I'm B, I can handle it. This is a small thing to a giant.

CHAPTER 11
MIA

Before I could get home I decided to call Blake. It had been
about a month since we had spoken to each other, but I
wanted to know how he felt now that the divorce was final.
Hello a deep voice said on the other end of the line. "Hey
Blake, I said with nervousness in my voice." "What's going on
Mia? How can I help you?" Blake really sounded like he didn't
want to talk to me but I forced the conversation anyways. "I
was calling to see if you had received the final decree and just
to talk to you about the whole situation. I know that
everything between you and I spiraled out of control quickly
and I just wanted to talk to you." "Okay, I'm listening, talk."
"Blake I know you probably don't believe that I loved you, but
I'm saying to you right now that I loved you with all my heart.
Your job, your job just consumed so much of your time and
you just wasn't the same person that I met. When I met you,

you constantly put me first and you cared about my feelings. Over a period of time I just felt like you didn't care anymore." "Look, Mia I've heard all of this bullshit from you so there's no need in going back in the past. I have moved on and obviously you moved on two years ago, so what the fuck do you want from me?" "I'm sorry Blake. I didn't call you to have a dispute. I just thought that we could talk civilized without any arguing or without any fussing and without any anger towards each other but I guess I was wrong. You seem to be very angry still and it's been two years." "So I guess I'm just supposed to forget about my wife, my life just because two years has passed? You were my world Mia. Sorry if a nigga didn't get over this shit as fast as you did. So how your other nigga doing?" "I really didn't call you to talk about him Blake, I called you to talk about us." "Us. You keep saying us, Mia, there's no fucking us. You ended us a long time ago." Before I could say anything else Blake ended the call. I lost my husband. I'm in love with a man that's in love with another man who also has infected me with the HIV virus. What else could go wrong in my life? I pulled up slowly to my two bedroom condo that Blake purchased for me. Even though I know I did Blake wrong and he probably hates me, Blake still looks out for my well-being. My alimony check every month was $7000. Blake paid for my condo and he also pays the note on my Mercedes. He really was a good man and I lost him. I lost him because I didn't have the time to support him and his dreams in making our life happy.

I looked at the phone and thought about calling Mia back, but I just couldn't muscle up enough energy. Even after all of this, I still loved her deeply. I decided to call my mom as she was the only one that I would talk to about this situation. "Hey, my beautiful mother. What you got going on?" "Hey, son. I was just telling your father that I haven't heard from you in a while. How are you?" "I'm still holding on despite everything that Mia and I are going through, that's actually why I called you. Mom, I still love her, mom I love her. What am I supposed to do?" "I know you love her baby. I raised you to be a good man. I raised you to respect women and to honor women and that's what you done for your wife. You haven't done anything wrong. Mia divorced you. Mia cheated on you. Mia moved on." "I know mom, I know. She just called me. I wanted to let you know that our divorce is final. I really couldn't talk to her. I really didn't have anything to say. Am I wrong for turning my back on my wife for not fighting for her?" "Baby, you can't fight for someone that's not fighting for you. Mia is moving in a whole other direction. You just have to continue to pray and ask God to lead your wife back to you." "I'm praying mom, I'm praying. I'm getting tired of praying. Speaking with her just then, she didn't even sound like she wanted to come back." "Baby don't you ever get tired of praying. Prayer changes things. God sits high and looks low. He knows what's going on and He'll fix it in His timing, not yours. It's something that's going on with Mia right now and God is not ready to bring her back. You have to accept that and trust in The Lord." I really wanted to just tell my mom everything that was going on but I didn't know what she would say if I told her that Mia left me for a man, that's in love with another man and that Mia is also HIV-positive. "Mom, I really appreciate the talk and I take everything that you're saying into consideration. Just continue to pray for me, you and Dad. I love you, goodbye." I had to disconnect the phone call with mom because I knew if I stayed on the phone any longer I would tell her the whole truth. I wasn't about to sit in the house, though. I decided to get dress and step out for a minute. After all that was going on with me and Mia, I decided to treat myself. I went and got me a new Maybach. I buzzed my driver when I was ready and decided to hit up one of the nightspots. To my surprise, it was plenty of fine women in the club tonight, on a Wednesday night, though. Must be my luck. I decided to have a seat at the bar, throwback a couple Patron shots and check out the scenery. Just when I decided to throwback my fifth shot of Patron I was approached by a gentleman. "What's going on man? Is anyone sitting right here?" "You good bro, I said. I didn't want to be rude so I extended my hand. "I'm Blake man. How you doing?" "What's up Homie, I'm Chase." "Nice to meet you man." "That's what's up." I loved this little spot, I knew everyone from the bouncers to the bartenders. "AJ let me get another shot of Patron man." "Damn Blake, that's your six shot right now bro." "I know man, hey, what can I say, female problems." AJ fixed me another drink while we discussed me looking for another partner in my business. "Look Blake, you might as well put your boy on. I need something better than this gig anyways." "Sorry to be ear hustling, Chase said, but what type of business are you in?" "No problem man. I own three of the biggest construction companies in the state of Florida. You might've heard of them, BCC, Incorporation." "Oh yeah, I've heard of them." "Well, my last partner got married and him and his wife decided to move overseas so I'm just looking for another partner, someone to invest into the company and help me run it." "Well, I actually have a degree in business and I run a construction company, been running it for the last two years, but I'm looking to start over. The company is just not ran the same since they've hired all these Mexicans and all." "I feel you Man. you got a business card. Chase pulled out a business card and gave it to me. Cool bro, I'll give you a call and maybe you can stop by the office." "Okay, that's a bet. Nice to meet you man, Chase said before walking off." "Now, how you gon play me for this nigga over here, AJ said laughing?" I looked at AJ cross eyed and said, "hit me with another shot nigga." "You better let me call yo drunk ass a cab." "Cab, nigga you must've forgot my name, nigga I got a driver, I said laughing at AJ. It is time for me to jet though my nigga. I'll get with you." "Shit, you better be trying to get at one of these hoes." "I'm good bro, I said dapping AJ."

CHAPTER 12
SHARON

My clock at work read 4 o'clock. I couldn't wait for 5 o'clock to get my weekend started. It was Friday and I had just about enough for the week. Everything seemed to drag by now every since I found out about Carter and his infidelity. Mia called me earlier this week and wanted to have coffee, but I blew her off so that I can have a real drink with her tonight. I don't know why I was so interested in Mia's relationship. Maybe I wanted to know that someone else's life is just as fucked up as mine. I called Carter's mother and asked her if she would get the boys this afternoon so that I could prepare my mind to go out and have a couple drinks with Mia, to my surprise, she said yes, so I decided to drop off the boys to her as soon as I got off. I needed to go to the mall and browse for me something sexy to wear. I pulled up to University Mall. Parts of the mall were still damaged from when Ivan hit. That was the only thing that

I hated about Florida the damn weather and all these tornadoes. I took my time browsing from store to store looking for the perfect outfit. I knew that Mia would be dressed to impress. I saved my favorite store for last, Ashley Stewart. If I couldn't find anything in here I knew I wouldn't be able to find anything. I grabbed a couple pretty pieces from the racks and went to the fitting room to try them on. I was twirling around getting my model on in the fitting room when I heard my husband's name coming from some woman's mouth. I stopped for a second so that I could continue to ear hustle. I tried to peep out of the side of the dressing room, but couldn't see anyone, I just heard voices. "Yes girl, Carter said that he is finally done with her and him and I will finally be moving on, said one of the women." "Girl, I don't see how you can play second best. He would have to be all in with me or nothing, you stupid." "Stupid. I'm far from stupid. I knew my position and I think I played it quite well." "Don't you feel bad? I mean you're sleeping with someone else's husband?" "I mean I felt bad when it first happened, but it's been going on for so long now I just can't stop it. I felt really bad when she called my phone and I had to tell her but, she was going to find out eventually. Carter definitely wasn't going to tell her so I just sped up the process." "Oh really, that's what you were doing, I said busting out the fitting room?" One of the women sat with her mouth wide open so I figured that she wasn't the one that was sleeping with my husband. Before I knew it I drew my hand back and punched the hell out of the other bitch. "So you think it's cool bitch to be sleeping with my husband and bragging about it, really?" Before I could mop the floor with her ass, the store attendants ran over to stop us. "Oh best believe it's not over bitch, when I catch you in the streets, I will be getting that ass, I said as I walked off." I didn't leave, however without paying for my bad fit. I was still going out tonight. Matter-of-fact, I felt even better after bopping that bitch in the face. I wanted to call Carter just so I can tell him that I ran into that bitch he was fucking but I said I'll let her tell him. He'll see it anyways, all over her face. Carter knows how I get down. Before walking out the store I turned around and glanced one more time at that bitch to let her know that it's on. Instead of putting in my normal gospel CD, I put in one of the CDs that Paris got me. I needed rap in my life right now. I wanted to call Paris to let her know what just happened but I hadn't even told her what was going on between Carter and I so I just decided to keep it to myself and go out tonight to meet Mia. Mia and I decided to meet up at Coconuts. This happened to be a favorite spot of mine and hers. Go figure. I'm surprised that we hadn't bumped into each other a long time ago. I got us a table and waited for her arrival. I liked to arrive early, so that I can feel out the scenery. I haven't been out in awhile, so I really wanted to get back in the groove of things before little miss prissy arrived. "How are you doing ma'am? Can I get you anything, the waitress asked trying to talk over the loud music?" "Yes, I'll take a strawberry margarita, please, and an order of wings, mild." "Be right up." "Thank you, I said as the waitress scurried away." I kept watching the entrance of the bar, but still no Mia. I reached in my bag to grab my phone and decided to give her a call but before I could call her she was tapping me on my back. "Hey girl." Girl, you scared the hell out of me. I was just about to call you." "I came in a few minutes ago but decided to go to the bathroom and primp a little before I came over. Well don't you look sharp, Sharon." "Thank girl. I try, I said being coy." The tan jumpsuit that I wore hugged me perfectly. I wasn't a big heel wearer, but I pulled out my orange snakeskin Brian Atwoods. "Sharon I can't believe that we never ran into each other. This is my favorite night spot. Nothing but gentlemen to cross your every path. Speaking of gentlemen, this is where I met my husband." I was glad that Mia brought up her husband, maybe she would continue our conversation from earlier this week. "When is the waitress coming over? I need me a drink." "She just left not too long ago. She should be back in a minute. I ordered us some mild wings and me a strawberry margarita." "I love margaritas, but I prefer a patron margarita. "Thanks for ordering some wings. I'm a little hungry myself." "So, you said this is where you met your husband, I asked to keep Mia talking?" "Yes. The year was 2001, right when this place started jumping." "Yeah, I remember girl." "So I was hanging out alone like I usually kick it and he joined me for a drink. After that night, the rest is history. We dated for 2 years and then got married." "Mia, if you don't mind me asking, what happened? From what I'm picturing, your husband was a decent guy. I mean nothing like mine." "Well." Before Mia could finish the waitress interjected. "Oh great, you're back. Can I have a patron margarita, hold the sour." "Yes ma'am." The waitress looked at me and asked if I needed anything else? I nodded her away. I was more interested in Mia's relationship. "Sorry girl. Where was I? Oh yeah, Mia answered her own question. So yeah, like my husband was very charming, a gentlemen. He catered to my every need, but when his company started to expand so did he. He was constantly out of town conducting business and all. If he wasn't out of town, he was working damn near 16 hours a day. Talk about kids, we barely had any time to conceive any, if you get what I mean. I know now that he was only trying to make a good life for us, but I guess my selfish needs got in the way. I'm truly sorry for what I put Blake through. Wait, I don't think I ever told you his name. It's Blake Bradford. I choked on my drink. "Blake Bradford, the multi-millionaire with the construction company, I asked eagerly?" "Yeah that's him. Do you know him, Mia asked?" "No, not personally that is, but my husband works for his company." "Really! Girl we have more in common than we thought, Mia said." Mia and I threw back plenty drinks and had plenty laughs. This was definitely what I needed. A friend, one that wouldn't judge me or my situation.

CHAPTER 13
PARIS

Bryan are you going to continue to ignore me, I mean I tell you I do not know where the band came from. Could you please give me a call when you get my message? I love you. This had to be the 6th voicemail that I had left Bryan and he still has not returned my phone call and I was beginning to get very frustrated. I decided to fold some clothes and do some chores until he finally return my phone call or send me a text message. I did wonder, however, why in the hell did "Silly" leave that club band in the trash can. I mean was he purposely trying to get me busted? Knowing him, he was trying to leave some type of mark. I guess so that I could be with him. Who knows? Everything in me wanted to call him though, and curse his ass out, but I could never cuss him out. He'll eventually be here and we will be tussling again and I really just

wanted to leave him alone.   While folding the clothes I heard
my phone going off. I ran to get it anticipating that it would
be Bryan. It was a text message from Bryan. "Hey, Paris. I'm
sorry about the way that I left. I really don't believe you and I
think we really need to talk about where our relationship is
going. I'll be back on Friday so that we can discuss our
future." I really didn't like the tone of his message. I did,
however, make up in my mind not to tell Bryan about my
escapade being that my fling was on his way back to prison
soon anyways.

"What's up girl?" "Hey boo. I've missed me some you, Amy
said, happy that Bryan called." "I got to tell you I was
surprised to see you pull down the job like that. At work you
sit back playing that good girl role. What's up with that?"
"Well, Bryan good girls are the biggest freaks or didn't you
know that?" "Yeah. I'm just saying it surprised me out of you
though. So what's been up?" "Just working and thinking
about what I want you to do to me the next time you're in
town." "Well, damn baby you about to find out." "What, Amy
said, slightly getting choked on her words?" "Yeah boo, I'm
outside." I saw her walk from the back peeping with them
sexy ass pants on. "Wait a second, I'm about to come out? I
waited on her and wondered how Paris would feel knowing
that I came up a whole day earlier and kicked it the whole time
with the chic from the movie store. Dismissing that thought, I
got my mind right for Amy. Nothing and I mean nothing will
prevent this wood from staying rock hard tonight. A part of
me was hurt though, because despite all the arguing and
bitching that Paris did, she really was a good woman. It's not
too many women willing to accept an ex-con, broke and with
not one but 2 kids. Paris even assumed responsibility for them
when my baby mamas would get on my ass. Shit. I can't even
believe I've taken it this far. I thought about really breaking it
off with Paris because she seemed to be the nutty type that will

kill a nigga if he done something like this and got caught. I mean over the past months she has accused me, but I think that she was trying to let me know that I didn't have to if I wanted to because she never had any solid proof of nothing I ever did. Shit, I could remember shortly a month after being with her, I went out and with her Fam, I fucked off. If she ain't mentioned that then I know she really don't know anything else. I felt bad that night too, because I went back to her and gave her the "d". Oh well. All's well that ends well. What guy fresh out the chain gang about to settle with one girl, not this one? Maybe one day though. "You ready baby, I asked when Amy got in?" Amy lived with her parents, so we had to get a room. I told her my financial situation, but unlike Paris, it didn't matter to Amy. She was willing to pay in order to spend time with a nigga. We talked on the way, really, just finishing off the long, all night conversations we had earlier in the week. I was glad when my baby mama called and interrupted. All her questions were killing my vibe. "Hello." "Bryan, I know you've been getting my texts. No need to ignore me because you have moved on. You know that I could care less. I feel sorry for the poor girl that got sucked in by you though. If only she knew." "Knew what Summer, that I'm a loving, caring gentlemen, and not to mention handsome." "Yeah and don't forget to add "father of the year." "Here you go. What you want Summer?" "Since you've been released Harmony has only seen you 3 times and on top of that Christmas is coming and she has her Christmas list ready. Do you plan on getting the things that I'm not getting?" "Damn, Summer you know I'm out of commission right now. I'll try." "Right, that means you are probably going to get that girl to buy everything."

Before Bryan could even respond, I hung up. I hated him for not being man enough to be a father to his daughter, his first born. I'm all that she has and need. Just to think that I wanted

to abort my child because of his trifling ass. Even after he
went to prison, I visited him and tried to make things work,
but then I found out about Lil Bryan and that Bryan was still
seeing his mother, also and writing and calling her too. I
finally let him go after years of cheating, lying and
manipulating. Bryan, in my eyes, died when I contemplated on
killing our child. One day I will sit Ms. Paris down and let her
know what she truly has on her hands because women of our
worth deserve better.

CHAPTER 14
MIA

I had been attending these weekly meetings for over 3 weeks and Sharon and I were bonding more than I imagined. She has helped me to realize my mistakes with Blake and I even helped her to visualize some areas where she may have gone wrong with Carter. The close of this meeting was unusual though. Our instructor asked us to write down all of our wants and fears. Our wants would be discussed and framed in a purple heart frame and our fears would be folded and stuffed in a purple inflated balloon and we would release the inflated balloons at the end of our next meeting. I never really put too much thought into my fears or my wants. To be honest, I just wanted to live without thinking, make moves without walking and forget my past while living it. Sounds weird, but to explain, I lived without making decisions first, whatever happens, happen. I made moves without even making a step because my ex-husband made it so that if I ever wanted anything, I could have it just by my name and living with HIV continuously made me a product of my past mistakes. As long as I had it, I lived in my past. What future could I possibly have? Sharon wanted to meet up after our meeting, but this assignment had me spazzed, so I declined. All the way home that evening I thought about my wants. I had everything I wanted and everything that I didn't want. I had my greatest fear in life so what could I possibly fear? Only a glass of wine, Benihana's, and R. Kelly's "Black Panties" CD would help me through the night. I was always amazed when I pulled up to my condo. It was absolutely amazing. It always made me think of Blake, however, since he was the reason I was able to sustain such a lifestyle. I grabbed my meal and entered my home. When I opened the door, I heard soft music playing and saw a silhouette of what appeared to be a man. I grabbed my phone to call 911 when I was instantly grabbed through the darkness. I yelled a frantic cry of help but a man silenced my yell by placing his hands around my mouth. "Shhh, a familiar voice said." "Blake, I grunted." He turned me around and I quickly slapped him. "Blake what in the hell are you doing scaring the shit out of me?" Laughing, "I'm sorry, he said. Calm down. Damn, I almost forgot how your small ass hands had major sting." He kept laughing as I closed the front door. I had forgotten that I had given Blake a key the last time that I was rushed to the hospital. He always respected my privacy, however, and I never imagined that he would pop over without notice. "So to what do I owe this spontaneous visit, I said, walking into the kitchen?" "Well, I have been an asshole lately and I wanted to express my sincere apology face to face and I figured that if I asked to come over that you would find a way to blow me off, which I could really use right now, if you feel me." "So you just come in my house, played music and lit candles and I'm suppose to woo all over you? I popped my bottle of Dom and cockily said, I don't think so." "Mia, I know you and you are just as happy to see me as I am to see you." "Oh, so you happy to see me? As I can recall, I was the biggest whore ever in our last convo." "Woman, I never said that you were a whore and I sincerely apologize if I made you feel like that. I was upset, pissed, disappointed. Shit, I was lost, Mia. I know you can understand. You're my world, my shining light. Fuck that, you're my wife." I looked up just in time to see tears forming in Blake's eyes. "Well, divorce or not, God says "Until Death Do Us Part," so as long as we both have breath in our bodies Mia, Blake said, grabbing me by my waist and breathing slowly just inches away from my lips, you are my wife and I am still your husband." Before I knew it we were tongue wrestling. Blake made me feel so special in that moment. We hadn't touched each other in over 2 years. My body quivered and my soft spot instantly moistened. Blake began to unzip my tight fitting BCBG scoop back dress. He slowly kissed the back of my neck while slowly unzipping my dress. The more the dress fell off the further the kisses went down my back. I didn't want to stop him. My body needed this, but I knew that Blake wasn't fully thinking his actions through. I had HIV and he didn't. Was my husband, ex husband, so willing to be pleased by me that he would jeopardize his own health? I moaned loudly, but I couldn't help asking, Blake what he was doing? "Shhhh, he said, placing one finger over my mouth before sticking it in my mouth, allowing me to caress it with my tongue. I know exactly what I'm doing. Let me take control. Relax. I got you." Blake always was a take charge man and that was one of the things that I fell deep in love with. Once I was completely naked, Blake scooped me up and took me to the bedroom. Candles were lit all over, even in the bathroom and to my surprise, "Black Panties" was already playing. My headboard was customized with a radio system in the center. Something inspired by Blake of course. Everything in our home was customized. We even had a flat screen television in the wall of our Jacuzzi. Blake stripped down to his black Versace briefs displaying his voluptuous penis. I couldn't believe this was about to happen. I definitely wanted and needed this. Blake disappeared in the darkness. He returned hiding something behind his back. Blake standing, tall in the shadows of the candles, reiterated the events from the night that we first met and concluded with the events from the night that he proposed to me. "Mia, will you marry me?" He grabbed my hand, kissed it and placed on it a 5 karat platinum, emerald cut, ruby engagement ring. I cried because, I knew Blake loved me. I knew he loved me from the first night that I met him. I'm so ashamed of what I done to him. Why didn't I consider counseling before falling weak to temptation? Before I could give Blake an answer to his proposal, Blake gently leaned on top of me kissing me lower and lower with every kiss. I could feel him getting closer to my hot spot. I place my hands on top of his head, pulling his dreads as he placed a small film around my vagina and licked in and out, round and round. Blake made my body explode with every bite, every suck. I moaned louder as I felt his tongue insert me. Blake was very careful not to make direct contact and I wasn't upset. I wanted to protect him as I always did. Blake emerged from down below, slid off his briefs and stroked his manhood, which stood at attention. He began to rub it across my lips before slowly inserting his rock hard into my mouth. I missed sucking on him. I was pleased, as well as him, every time I gave him pleasure. Blake pulled out and slipped on a Trojan Natural Lamb condom. Blake was allergic to latex and I hated condoms so I was glad when we decided to stop using them all together. I wrapped my legs around Blake's back and moaned with every thrust he gave. "Daddy, I missed you, I continuously chanted. Please forgive me? Please forgive me?" Blake didn't respond , he just kept paining me. He flipped me over as soon as "Legs Shakin" started playing. I loved this song and never made love to it, so this moment was indeed special and I was honored to be sharing it with my husband, ex husband. Blake wrapped my hair around his hand and forced pain from the back. He knew that I loved it this way. I continued to throw it back at him. He smacked my ass asking "who it belongs to?" I moaned "you, you daddy," as he kept pushing inside of me." Blake was the only man that could make me orgasm back to back. "Awe baby, you ready, Blake asked?" "I'm ready baby. I'm ready." He continued to breathe harder and pumping faster. I knew he was about to orgasm and with my last throw back, we came together. I absolutely loved when we met each other's orgasm. This was the first time that I had made love in a long time. Chase never took his time and the mere fact that he wanted it from the back as much as I did used to turn me off. I laid across Blake's chest as he held me way into the night hours. The candles had burnt all the way down and the music had stopped. Blake snored all night. I eventually fell asleep and became totally annoyed to hear my alarm going off. "Blake, Blake baby, hit the alarm." He was still knocked out. I rolled over, hit the alarm and rolled back onto an empty wet spot. Did he leave, I wondered rubbing my eyes? Suddenly I realized that all of last night was a dream when I didn't see that big rock on my hand. I smiled because I finally figured out my assignment. I grabbed my Bible off of my nightstand. Something that Blake said in my dream was weighing heavily on my heart and I wanted to research it. One thing about my husband, ex-husband, is he never speaks about The Bible and not visually pinpoint it for you. I went to the Book of Corinthians because it's the Book of Love. To my surprise, Blake had bookmarked 1 Corinthians 7. I began to read it and was blown away when I read verse 10. It stated, "And if you are married, stay married. This is the Master's command, not mine. If a wife should leave her husband, she must either remain single or else come back and make things right with him. And a husband has no right to get rid of his wife." I continued to read the entire chapter and was astonished again when I got to verses 39-40. It stated, "A wife must stay with her husband as long as he lived. If he dies, she is free to marry anyone she chooses." Blake was right. As long as we were both still living we were husband and wife and I wanted my husband, "Till Death Do Us Part," and "He Ain't Dead Yet."

CHAPTER 15
PARIS

During the time of Bryan's absence, I cleaned and cleaned until it was nothing left to clean. Cleaning was my way of dissolving the problem. My way of sweeping dust under the rug. With Bryan, that tactic worked and I hoped that he was willing to come eat, have sex and cum again and again. He was still sending me to voicemail, but I was expecting him any moment now since he did take the efforts to text "I'm on my way." He could be so juvenile at times but with a little more time I was eager to tame him. It was a Friday night and I had been reading an article entitled "Loving Ourselves." It was very interesting and some valid points really stuck out to me, but the reality of it, I wasn't ready to face the true facts about my life. I just wanted the pieces to fall in place. One interesting thing mentioned, however, was "...moreover, if we can't love ourselves, we will look for others to love us, in hopes that if they give us enough love our unlovable parts will diminish or get better. Unfortunately, we will tend to attract others who cannot love or accept themselves either, thus setting ourselves up for even more hurt or disappointment." I began to ponder on my past relationships. Jorese didn't display the actions of love towards himself and William committed suicide. There was no way that William could've loved himself. So did I not love myself? Based off of this article, like attracts like. But I did love myself, didn't I? That article frustrated me and began to ruin my night before it even began. Bryan didn't have a job, but he didn't mistreat me. He had a past, but so did I. I would say that Bryan loved himself, so even if I didn't love myself in the past, I was definitely on track now, except for the fact that I wasn't faithful to Bryan. I really did feel like Bryan was seeing someone else when I dipped out on him but I didn't have proof. I'm a gut buster. If I get the feeling 9 times out of 10, I'm running with it. I decided to lie down and clear my mind for a minute and before I knew it, I was well into a 3 hour nap when Bryan called. "Paris, come open the door." Bryan's tone sounded aggravated but maybe I was still sleepy. "Hey, I said, reaching to hug him." "What's up, he said, walking right pass me." I just rolled my eyes and closed the door. This is going to be a long night and just to think Christmas was right around the corner. "Bryan are you ready to talk about this? It's been weeks now and you have yet to discuss it or talk to me for that matter." "Paris it's really nothing to say, but during our separation and the mere fact that I'm not financially stable, our relationship has run its course." "What. You came all the way here just to tell me that. You could've done that shit from a pay phone. On top of how I've been there for you." I just stood still. I couldn't say anything else because deep down I was wrong. I cheated and even though I accused him, I didn't have any proof, so there was no need in defending the fact that we should ultimately stay together. "You know what Bryan, you're right.

We've only been together for a short period of time and we can't seem to get it right, so maybe stepping back will do our relationship some good." I breathed heavily. Relieved that Paris agreed. This wasn't going to be as hard as I imagined and fact was Paris didn't even know about Amy. "So are we in agreement that the relationship has just dissolved and maybe in the future we can pick things back up, I asked, slightly pissed that Bryan had me waiting this long." "Agreed, Bryan said. One question though Paris." "What's that baby?" Bryan started playing Plies "One Mo Time". Laughing I said, "hell yes." No matter our arguments Bryan and I had great sexual chemistry and it wasn't any sense in not getting a piece before we decided to part.

The sun beaming through the windows and the voracious sound of the doorbell woke me up. Damn, I had forgotten that my mom was scheduled to arrive this morning. Jacarious had a scheduled procedure on Monday and she decided to come a couple days earlier. I knew this was about to be weird. Bryan and my mom really didn't get along, but at least Bryan would be leaving on Monday after we left for Children's Hospital. "Hey mom. I'm glad you got here safely, I said, yawning and grabbing her bags. "Paris, how are you? Where are my grand boys?" "They are in the room mom." I got her settled and went back in the bedroom to discuss with Bryan about his departure. "Babe, are you awake?" Sarcastically he said, "no Paris. I was waiting on you to ask me am I awake." "Very cute. Well, my mom just arrived and I was thinking can we at least get along until I leave on Monday?" "I'm good baby." "You sure are, I said winking." "I'm going to get breakfast ready. Please get dressed and come out and be cordial. Thank you."

I was so thrilled when Monday morning arrived. This had been one long weekend, however Bryan made it a little more comfortable by being gone most of the day hours. I didn't question what he was doing, but I made for damn sure he didn't do it in my shit. He took his own beat up Cadi and I enjoyed my mother and prepared my son for his procedure. Jacarious was scheduled for a bladder augmentation. Due to the car accident, Jacarious's bladder stopped growing and he was suffering from chronic bed wetting. No matter how many times he would urinate, he constantly had wettings in between times when he shouldn't. This procedure was definitely something that would give Jacarious a little more independence and it should be a major factor with his self-esteem. I know that he hated being his age and still had accidents, but Dr. Silar assured us that this procedure should definitely fix the problem. We we're running late, but I did have a chance to talk to Bryan and make sure that we were in agreement on the separation and that he was clear on how to lock up the house once he was done packing.

"What's up girl?" I decided to call up Amy after Paris left this morning. "Look, you know today is my last day up here, right?" "How was I suppose to know that Bryan?" "Well, Paris and I decided to take a break on this so called relationship." "You mean engagement." "Look, chill out with that smart ass mouth. I hate that shit. Let a nigga talk without interrupting, I snapped. Anyways, I'm calling to see if you wanted to see me before I headed down the way to the F.L.A." "You can't come to my parents house Bryan and I used all the money I had on the last room that we got. So unless you got funds to accommodate our chilling, I guess we got to take a rain check." "Shit, shit, shit. I really wanted to see you girl. Well, you could. Nawl, never mind. I know you ain't with nothing like that." "What?" "Well, I was gon say you could come here. I mean Paris is gone and won't be back until next week sometime." "Bryan you sure about that? I mean that's her house you asking me to come up in." "Look, you good.

I'll text you the address. Get dress and come in about an hour." Amy hung up and I immediately started regretting the fact that I invited her. This was more low down than when I fucked them hoes that night with Paris cousin. I finished packing and went and made Paris a CD of all my favorite songs that I recorded while we were together. I actually dropped a tear. I did love her, but I wasn't ready to be settled down with one woman yet.

CHAPTER 16
SHARON

Weeks turned into months before I ultimately decided that I was ready to bask in the presence of my husband. Carter nearly destroyed our family and I was anticipating his reaction to all of this chaos that he had caused. It was the weekend and the boys had their games so I determined that this would be the best ice breaker for Carter and me. The boys really wasn't buying the excuses I was rendering them and the fact remained that they really missed their father. The morning of the game I got up extra early to prepare for our reuniting. Carter asked if I could come over to Mema's and pick him up. Mema was the name that the boys acquired for their Paternal grandmother. Due to the stress of my marriage and bearing on the responsibilities of a full-time employee and mother, I had lost tons of weight. I wasn't used to it, but I decided to show off just a little to show Carter that his newbie wasn't comparable. Upon arriving, I peeked at my boys in the back seat. They sat with such excitement on their faces. I detested more than anything how much this was affecting them. Tears began to form in the niches of my eyes as I blew for Carter to come out. I quickly wiped them away as I saw him, however. Wow! Carter's body was dreamily amazing. I don't know if it's been the time apart or if I was drunk in love, but everything about him was standing out. His walk was a slow strut, a precise duplicate of Denzel Washington in the movie "Training Day," and if I'm not mistaken, I noticed him licking his lips just like LL Cool J did. I tried not to stare, but Carter's body was too appealing. I started to moist underneath as I thought about our countless sexual escapades. Carter had the tools to fulfill all of my body's desires. I felt like I matched him stroke for stroke, hence that's why it was undeniably able for me to fathom his cheating, but I learned through the program that it wasn't my fault and that I didn't do anything to cause my husband's infidelity, however it was his own inabilities to be the man that I deserved that made him flee. Knowledge is power and I was learning all that I could while holding out the limitless sessions at Heel My Heart. "Daddy, daddy, the boys yelled as they jumped up at their father." He embraced them tightly and for a moment I thought that I saw tears form in his eyes. This endeavor was one of the principal reasons why I was blessed that I had sons instead of daughters. Any situation is hurtful to kids, however, as a woman, I wouldn't want my daughter to witness this kind of hurt that a respectable woman could experience from her husband. I didn't want my boys to think that this is how a woman should be treated either, but boys by nature are closer to their mom and I knew if it was anything other than education that I should instill in them it was respect. "Hello Sharon. Thanks for coming to get me. How have you been?" "Despite our situation, I've been hanging in there. The boys need me, you know." Our conversation was kind of dry on the ride to the field but, I was happy that the boys' game brought us closer. We shared a common love for sports and the mere fact that our boys had been playing since before they could hold a bottle straight was an added bonus.

"Hey Sharon, would you like something from the concessions?" "No thank you Carter." I ran off to the concessions quickly when I saw Shannon standing by the gates. What the hell was she doing out here, I thought? She knew that Sharon was accompanying me today, but young girls are so stupid and full of damn drama. She couldn't wait until she could rub the baby bump in Sharon's face after Sharon popped off on her at the store. Although Sharon didn't tell me about it, Shannon did and she even wanted to press charges after she found out that she was pregnant shortly after the incident happened. Everything in me convinced her otherwise including threatening to leave her alone as a single mother if she tried any bullshit but here she pops today. I guess she thinks that I won't leave her, but she had another thing coming if she thought that I would allow her to hurt my family anymore than she already had. Today was my opportunity to mend my marriage and become the father that I knew I could be to my boys. All Sharon ever wanted was for me to assume responsibilities as a man and to honor, protect and respect her. I never meant to get Shannon pregnant, well I never meant to, shit I guess I did since I'm fully aware of how to make a baby. "What the fuck do you think you're doing, I yelled snatching Shannon by the arm?" "Oh, so I guess I'm not your trophy anymore, huh Carter? Guess this baby bump blows up your whole fairy tale ass life, huh? Well I'm pregnant and I deserve all of your time. You don't have time to play hubby anymore. Leave her and come with me or I will tell her about our love child." The more and more Shannon rolled her neck yapping her mouth, the angrier I got. "Look bitch, I don't care about that shit you talking. Get the fuck from out here or your ass will pay." Shannon began to cry. "Oh, I love you Shannon. I will never leave you Shannon. You're more special to me than anyone Shannon. Guess all of those were lies? I gave up school for you. I disrespected my family for you. Shit, I took a punch in the face from your wife and now I'm carrying your child and this is the best that you can give me. Do I really deserve this Carter? You're a ruthless bastard and I pray that your wife realize how undeserving you are of her forgiveness and love." Before I could say anything, Shannon stormed away. I glanced at my phone and noticed that Sharon had texted me twice. I ran back to the stands totally forgetting that I told her that I was going to the concessions. "Hey babe. Sorry it took me so long." "So where's your stuff?" "The line was too damn long so I left." Lie after lie. I was tired of lying and hurting my wife and kids. "God, give me a sign of what to do? Who should my loyalty go to?" I was hurting two women and now I have another child that's about to come out of my web of deceit. I grabbed my wife's hand and kissed it and placed my arm around her as we cheered our boys on for the rest of their games. I loved the feeling that I got from my wife but I hated her always putting me down because I loved smoking weed or hanging out with the boys all the time. I wasn't a deadbeat. I went to work every day and took care of my family financially but she complained about me always being too high to play with the boys or help them with homework assignments. It wasn't much that she was asking and the way Sharon loved me, despite that little whore telling her about our affair, I knew that I wanted to change and be the man that my wife deserved. I would take care of my outside child and hope that once I told

Sharon that we would be in a state of bliss and she would forgive my last indiscretion and we could live our life happily ever after.

CHAPTER 17
PARIS

10,9,8,7,6,5,4,3,2,1 Happy New Year. My boys and I
celebrated our New Year in Children's Hospital. Although it
wasn't the traditional, I was happy to see a new year and
blessed to have my son come out of surgery and to be
recovering well. My mom had left a couple of days earlier to
avoid traffic and Jorese had to get back also. Despite his
absence in the kids' lives, I was happy to see that he came to
our son's surgery. Jacarious could be a real butt when it came
to getting shots and all and he became quite fond of his
father's presence when they were administered. Jorese could
keep Jacarious calm, unlike me, I would just ask the nurses to
leave while Jacarious and I just hold each other and cry, but
this procedure had to be done and Jorese presence was even
calming me. Jacarious did not want to have the tube placed
down his throat. He fought and yelled and even spit at the

doctor. They gave us a minute with him, but Jacarious still wouldn't allow the doctor to do his job. Jorese then said, "watch Jr. Watch Papa take the tube down. I promise you that it won't hurt." I couldn't believe that Jorese were about to do this but he did. He took the tube like a champ and not only did he convince Jacarious, but the entire room full of spectators as well. Jacarious was convinced and they rolled him down. I sat and cried and Jorese began to console me. At first I was resistant because Jorese was involved and even though Bryan and I decided to call it quits, I still loved him. "This is the time that you two should be there for one another, my mom said. Let that man console you. That's your son together and he needs both of his parents right now." I knew that my mom was right, but it felt wrong and good at the same time. Something about Jorese touch made me shiver. "Hey mom, can we go to the game room, Jacarious interrupted my thoughts?" The best part about this hospital was the game room, next to the awesome staff and food. It was late, but since it was New Years I decided to go party with the boys. I waited to see if Bryan would text me, but it was almost 1 in the morning and still no text or phone call. We had been talking ever since he left, but it was strange that he wouldn't contact me today. I decided to text him, but got no response. I text him again, still no response. I text Bryan up to 4 a.m. with no response. I dozed off as I heard my boys snore in the background. I couldn't help but cry a little because I knew why Bryan wasn't answering. It was obvious that he was with a woman. I didn't mention it to him, but one night while Bryan was in one of his studio sessions, I went through his phone and it was plenty women in his phone that had Atlanta numbers and I only knew of one family member that he had up here and her name was not Amy, Red, Tammy or Nicole. One in particular, Amy, had the same area code as my number so I figured that she must live in my area or very near. I wanted to ask him, but I knew he would lie so I didn't even bother. The mere fact that Bryan would be cheating on me with someone that lived in Atlanta was bad but to think that she lived in Henry County that was fucking with me. The morning bright sun woke me. It wasn't like I got any rest because I tossed all night. I grabbed my phone and quickly skimmed through the missed calls and messages. One of them was from Bryan. It was a text that read, "Hey Nikki. This Kash. Bryan allowed me to keep his phone for the night because my girl broke mine and I needed it for an emergency. He said to call him at the house." I rolled my eyes. Why in the hell would Bryan leave his phone with Kash and not tell me before he done so as if me calling would not be an emergency? I called the phone and to my surprise, Bryan answered. "So I just read a text from Kash that said he had your phone. Let me guess, you got up super early and drove to Georgia to get it, right?" "Happy New Year's Paris. Good morning Paris. Damn. You always down a nigga back and why, didn't you say it was over? Shit. I'm entitled to miss every damn phone call and text if I wanted to. News flash, I'm S.A.F., Single As Fuck, so miss me with the questions. Kash actually just left. He drove here last night after things between him and Keisha got out of hand and that's how I got my damn phone. Calm down baby."

Bryan never really talked to me this way but I guess he was learning that "my man" must put his foot down. Well, my ex-man must put his foot down. He was right. I did in fact say that we should take a break, but we left on such good terms and had been talking ever since so I figured things were still accordingly, but Bryan showed me a different side of him. "Look, Bryan I thought that maybe we would still be close until." "Until what Paris, until you was good enough to move on? I'm not a toy. Paris can't pick me up and put me down when I get dirty. You either in or out." Silence fell over the line. I didn't want to answer Bryan, because I really did want to keep him around until I no longer needed his presence.

"Just like I thought. Paris it's over. Not really much we can talk about. You made up your mind now deal with it." Bryan hung up before I could say anything else. Just before I could cry, I heard the boys yawning. It's a new year and Bryan was right. I wanted out because I deserved better and that's definitely what I was going to wait for.

CHAPTER 18
MIA

For the past couple of nights all of my dreams were about Blake and to my surprise I didn't once think about Chase. It was early Saturday morning and I had a spa date. I faithfully got my Brazilians, manis, pedis and full body massages. During my session I scheduled brunch with a couple of friends. I could really go for a ménage of mimosas. Right before getting my massage I decided to text Blake. "Hello Blake. You have been on my mind constantly. I'm having brunch with a couple of my Sorors within the next couple of hours. I was wondering, if you weren't busy, would you wish to accompany me to Tampa for a weekend getaway. We truly need to talk and I was thinking that we could have dinner at one of our favorites, Ocean Prime. Please let me know something at your earliest convenience." I laid back, plugged my ears and allowed Tyrese to serenade me as my therapist went in. I knew it was a brave move to text Blake out of the blue and to ask him to "run away," with me, but as The Bible says, "you have not, cause you ask not," soooo I was willing to accept whatever he said, even if it was a rejection. Finally done with everything, I headed over to one of my favorite spots for brunch, The Grand Marlin. This place had an awesome view. Blake and I used to come here a lot for dinner and watch the sun set while tossing back Patron Margaritas. I especially loved that they had valet parking because me plus 6 inch heels equaled no long walking. "Hello, Mrs. Bradford. What a pleasure for you to join us today." I smiled at the valet and strutted along. I loved the fact that I was still recognized as Mrs. Bradford no matter where I went in Pensacola, Tampa or Jacksonville. Blake's construction companies earned us grave recognition in all three cities. He was definitely the man and face it, I was definitely the woman, his woman, and every woman envied that. Our divorce didn't go viral because Blake was very private and he made sure all paparazzi was paid off and since he had a couple of judges in his pocket from way back when he was dealing, our public records wasn't exactly public. Of course I was the first to arrive. My Sorors were on w.i.g.t. time, when I get there and I hated that, but at least I had time to wait for Blake's response with no interruptions. My girls could be so judgmental and I didn't want their input on my decision to fraternize with Blake again. I stared at my cell and noticed it had been 2 hours since I had text Blake. What business did he have early on a Saturday morning? Even though I committed adultery Blake remained faithful to God, his vows and me, but a part of me thought that maybe he had slipped. Usually he responds quickly with a short, smart ass response but not today. I began to dial his number when the waitress startled me. "Good morning Mrs. Bradford. Will you be having your usual to get started?" "Hello Catherine. You're glowing as usual and yes of course, I'll have a Mimosa. Have you by chance seen any of my usual party?" Catherine began to chuckle. "You mean the "never on time, crew," no Hunty, I haven't." I picked up my cell to call Blake again as I laughed at Catherine and this time I was interrupted by an incoming text from my Soror Suzette. "Hey booski, Jerard came in town last night. Please don't be mad, but I needed this loving lol, smiley face, smiley face. Rain check." Just like one of us to cancel for wood. I couldn't help but smile because I would've cancelled in a heartbeat, especially if I had a drought like Suzette. Catherine came back just in time with my mimosa. "Right on time lovely, I said as Catherine added my two cherries to the top. I'm one down, two to go, I said, as Catherine rubbed my shoulder and shook her head." I slowly sipped on my mimosa when I saw the name that I had been waiting on flash across my screen. "Hello Mia. Sorry for such a late response. I had a business meeting this morning and guess where, Tampa. I guess it was God ordained for us to meet, huh. Well, I'm wrapping things up here and you know how I hate for you to drive all alone and especially at night so wrap it up with the ladies and head my way. BTW tell the ladies I said hello and I'm really glad that you reached out to me. ~Husband" "Yasssss, I yelled." I decided to pull a Suzette on Kelis and Dreia. "Hey ladies, I've been waiting for half an hour now and Suzette just cancelled so I will let you ladies do Who you are doing and we will get up when I come back to town. Oh yeah, I had an important meeting to come up so I'm leaving town for a couple of days. Talk to you soon. Ciao Bellas, smiley face, Mia." I signaled to Catherine, gave her a $50 bill and headed towards the entrance. Catherine was my favorite waitress and I always made sure that she was tipped beyond reality sometimes. She worked here part-time and was a full-time student in pursuit of a Masters in Communications and I always believed in building my sisters up so I kept her Michael Kors filled whenever I could. I respected that she chose a respectable income versus doing something strange for a piece of change. Don't get me wrong, I supported the naked hustle and I definitely wasn't one to judge, but I was glad that Catherine didn't choose that road. She had a mini me that adored her and it was good that she didn't expose her to a "getting a dollar no matter what," attitude. She was always grateful for my tips. She would always leave a napkin folded with a pen drawn heart with the initials CB at the end. "Leaving already Mrs. Bradford," the valet said as he opened the door for me? "You know me, always on the go. See you next time."

I thought about all the things that I wanted to get before heading to Tampa and the main thing that came to mind was something black in lace. I headed over to Vickie's before I went home to pack. I didn't know how long I would be staying or what we would be doing, except for dinner tonight at Ocean Prime, so I overly packed for all occasions. I was finished packing by 1 and my tank was filled. I got on 10 and headed towards Tampa. Instead of driving the 550, I rented a Jaguar. Men were always intrigued by the unexpected and I was ready to deliver in this Jag Hunty. Not to mention, I splurged a little on a new Louie bag and some new Louboutins. Blake was about to see a new and fiercer Mia. The 7 hour drive was bananas, but I was happy to finally reach my destination. Blake had called several times during my drive to check on me and to let me know that he had us booked at the regular, Embassy Suites on Westshore. I mean Blake was the contractor of this beauty so we got unlimited stays of course. Aside from being free, it was one of the nicest hotels in Tampa. I was greeted the same way as I was greeted by the valets in Pensacola. As I said everywhere I go.... yeah, you know the rest but please don't get it twisted with Pac baby. The Bellhop grabbed my luggage that was packed for a month and escorted me to the top floor of course. Once I was all nestled in I called Blake to let him know of my arrival. He had to run back to the office, but I was ecstatic to see how Blake had romanced out our suite. Flowers were everywhere with petals on the bed and candles lit up the Jacuzzi. Beside the Jacuzzi sat an iced filled bucket with a bottle of Dom and an engraved wine flute. I closely examined it and it was my exact flute from our wedding day. Blake timed my arrival perfectly as he always did because the bubble filled Jacuzzi was still steamy. "Hello. I'm here. Well, actually I've been here for about an hour. I just wanted to indulge in this well romanced pad. Glad to know that you haven't forgotten just what it takes." "I will never forget what it takes to please my dear Mia and don't you ever forget it Little Lady. Look, I'm already dressed so get ready and I'll send a car over to get you. We have dinner reservations for 10. I also have a surprise for you so hurry, dear." I hung up blushing from ear to ear. Blake never ceased to amaze me. All of this and he has a surprise for me too. This was going better than I imagined. Just months ago he was chomping me off and now it's like we are husband and wife again. I made sure that I was dressed to undress. Blake called again when I got in the car to say that something happened at the office and that he would arrive about 10 minutes late for dinner. I began to feel a sense of discomfort. This was the exact reason I felt unloved and unappreciated and why I ended up in the arms of Chase. I hadn't thought about Chase in a while and since he was chomping me off too, I decided to give him some space. I did, however, decide to text him to see what's been up.

I stared at the text from Mia asking if I was doing ok since we hadn't talked in awhile. I had taken up a new job and was traveling a little bit more and I had even broken it off with ol' dude. I was actually kind of missing her and had all intentions of reaching out to her when I got back in town so it was odd that we were both thinking about each other at the same time. I quickly text her back. "Hey You. Glad to hear from you. I hope you know that I'm regretful about how I've been treating you and I really have some things that I want to talk to you about. I truly miss you and as soon as I get back in town I will call you. ~Love C." "Hey man. Are you ready," my colleague asked as I quickly shut my phone? "Yeah. Let's ride. I was just closing an old deal that has to be settled when we get back."

I smiled as I read Chance's response. I replied back with a simple smiley. Looks like both of these men were feeling Ms. Mia, but hey, I'm not mad. The driver pulled up to the restaurant and I couldn't believe that Blake and I was minutes away from reuniting. This dinner had to go perfect. I went to powder my face and make sure that my boobs was sitting up just right in my XO Collection dress. I glanced in the mirror again before leaving the restroom and saw perfection. I slowly walked back to our table and noticed two men sitting. I could see Blake, but I didn't know who the other gentleman was. Blake stood as I got closer. He grabbed me and said "hey, man I would finally like to introduce you to my lovely wife, Mia Bradford." The strange guy turned to face me and I nearly fainted. It was Chase. What in the hell was going on? Chase extended his hand with just about the same expression as mine. "Hi Mia. It's great to finally meet you."

CHAPTER 19
PARIS

I was so glad when they finally discharged Jacarious. This had been a very long road but once again it was a road that we triumphed. I was surprised to see an incoming call from Bryan as we were driving home. "Paris, baby, I miss you and I'm sorry for responding the way I did a couple of days ago. Do you forgive me?" Bryan always wanted something when he apologized out of the blue but this time he seemed to be very sincere. I listened with no interruptions and to my surprise, he never asked for anything except could I call him once I was settled at home with the kids. I agreed. I was so relieved to be home in my bed and I know the kids were relieved as well.

They didn't waste anytime before running upstairs to play the Wii. It was a Christmas gift and they only had a couple of days to break it in so they were ecstatic about playing. Looking around the house I noticed that Bryan had cleaned up and nicely may I add. He even changed the sheets and bedcovers in our bedroom. The bathroom was clean and even the kitchen. On my nightstand I noticed a CD with my name on it and a little message, "Our love will forever be ~Bryan." I popped it in and listened to all of the songs that Bryan had recorded for me the duration of our relationship. Even the very first song, which he recorded days after we met. All of the songs were old except the very last one. It was entitled "Agape." Bryan must have recorded it right before he left. I begin to tear up and wondered if I made a mistake by breaking it off. I dozed off listening to the music. I didn't realize how tired I was until I woke up 3 hours later. I prepared dinner for the boys and decided to give Bryan a call. "Heyy Baby, Bryan literally song." "Well don't we sound happy to hear from me? I'm glad that you apologized for your actions and I truly appreciate the CD. I listened to it from beginning to end. It had me reminiscing on all of our good times. We really did have some good times Bryan." We talked for almost an hour when Bryan had to go. I couldn't believe before ending the call Bryan said the infamous "I Love You." I felt all bubbly inside again even though I knew that Bryan was in a bad place to be my husband and that's indeed what I was looking for.

"What's up Amy? I knew she was mad from the text messages she had sent when I was on the phone with Paris. I ignored at least 10 calls from her and based off of her last text I knew I had to end the phone call with Paris even though I didn't get to ask what, what I really wanted. "Oh, what's up. What in the hell Bryan. I called you over 30 times. What in the hell is funny?" I laughed at the fact that women could be so extra. She didn't call me no damn 30 times but just like a woman she had to exaggerate so that her anger could coincide with the situation. If a man didn't answer 40 seconds ago, what makes women think that he's going to answer every 40 seconds after that. Example if he's in the shower for 10 minutes and a woman call every 40 seconds, shit that's almost 12 missed calls right there. "Nothing baby. I just want you to calm down. I was in the shower. I left my phone on the charger so that it would be charged when you called. It had been off the charger all day. I was thinking about you and this is how you treat me." "Okay so when you saw my missed calls and texts why didn't you call me? It's been almost an hour." "When I got out the shower, I went out back in the studio and played around and lost track of time. By the time I was coming back in, you were calling. Everything has been great. We spent New Year's together and we will be together this weekend. Let's not fight already. I think I'm falling in love with you. Don't leave me Amy?" "I'm not baby. I just don't want to lose you. I do love you and I don't want to cause you the same problems as that last girl. I'm good for you and I will never belittle you. We will build together." I hated that I was still stringing these two women around. It was an addiction. I had to be with different women all of the time. "Amy I know that you are the woman for me. You have always had my back ever since we started kicking it. I do have some bad news though." "What's wrong baby?" "I'm not going to be able to chill with you, well I'm not able to come up there because my car is torn up. It will take $200 to fix it. Will you be able to come here instead?" "Babe I told you that my mom is taking my car out of town this weekend. I don't have any other way." I could hear the exasperation in Amy's voice. I really needed her this weekend so I did the unbelievable. "Baby do you have the $200 to let me borrow until next week. I really need for you to be with me this weekend. I miss you." I was surprised to hear her say yes. This girl really trusted me, unlike Paris. I guess I could give this relationship thing with her a try. Maybe she could change me. I had been out of prison for a minute now and done smashed everything walking by. I knew what Paris had to offer and I knew that marriage was on her mind so I'm not going back in that trap but I couldn't tell her out right. I had to gently slip away. Even though Amy was sending me the money, I needed more money to take out the dime I met at the mall yesterday. I had all intentions on getting the money from Paris for the car but since Amy was sending it I would get play money from Paris. It was late in the night and I knew Paris was sleep so I texted her. "Hey baby. I really enjoyed our talk earlier and I know that I still love you. I really want to come see you this Sunday. I got to come handle some biz and then I'm right back out. The only problem is my car is acting up. Could you send me $200 to get it fixed. I know that we have had our ups and downs but I feel like we are soul mates plus I miss your wetness. Big B has been real lonely lately without your touch and I know you miss him. Call me in the morning and we can finish discussing Sunday. I love you." If this don't work, I don't know what will. Paris was definitely feeling our last talk and since she was deep in her emotions and quite vulnerable I knew that she would send it and let me come smash.

When I awoke the next morning I noticed a text from Bryan. A part of me tingled. Money. Did he really have the nerve to ask me for money? My stomach began to bubble as I pondered over Bryan's message. Usually when this happens something is definitely wrong. Intuitions was something I always had but rarely acted on for fear of my insecurities coming to reality. Before I knew it, I had text him back "Yes. I'll send it right away. See you Sunday." Maybe I wanted the sex, maybe I knew that Bryan was playing me but I wanted to see him so I ignored that gut feeling. The Sunday that Bryan plan to drop by I made sure to have a nice dinner, my candles, wine and some sexy lingerie ready. I was about to put something on him. I waited all day. Bryan text me sporadically to let me know that he was waiting on his homie to come by so that he could ride with him. All day had passed by and night soon fell and Bryan still hadn't arrived. I thought about calling him but something stopped me. I guess it was the fear of him not answering but I realized that I had the same feeling that I had when I read his text. Something wasn't right. Midnight came and still no Bryan. The last time that I heard from him was around 6 saying that he was leaving Florida. He should've been here by now. I decided to call him and he didn't answer. I called again and he didn't answer. I waited for a couple minutes and called again, still no answer. Before I could dial again, Bryan text me. I read it with anger and disgust. I was so hurt. "I'm with her. Stop it." I didn't know how to respond. Who was her? Why did he lie to me? Most of all, why did he use me?

CHAPTER 20
SHARON

Carter had been amazingly supportive since his return. Our relationship had really deepened and I was so glad to be in his comfort again. The boys really enjoyed him and he even supported them with all of their homework and activities at school. Carter had done a 180. Every morning before I left for work or before Carter left for work we said a prayer together and we said a prayer with the boys. On Sunday morning we all attended church service. Carter even began to get involved with the other men in the church. Our pastor and First Lady were very supportive in helping us to rebuild our marriage. Even though I was aware of Carter's infidelity I decided that family comes first and that I will support my husband and all of his endeavors. We all make mistakes and I was willing to forgive Carter for all of his indiscretions. At this moment the only thing that would be unforgivable would be of course, if he fathered a child and me knowing that Carter didn't want anymore kids he definitely wouldn't be that careless. I couldn't even fathom the thought of Carter fathering a child with another woman, however, I did have it in the back of my mind that this could have happened. Since Carter's return I decided to stop going to Heel My Heart. For one, I didn't want Carter to know where I was going and for two I felt like I no longer desired help of this organization. My marriage was going to work and I was determined to make it happen no matter the cost. On my way to work I noticed a text from Mia. Since I haven't been to the class in weeks now I knew that I would finally hear from her. Mia and I really hit it off and we continued our friendship inside and outside of the class. I really wasn't ready to let her know that Carter and I was rekindling our marriage. We were associates, but I wouldn't yet, call us friends. Once I snuggled in my office, I read her text. "Hello doll. I'm just checking with you. Haven't heard from you in a minute. Get back with me. Ciao Mia. (Heart). Mia always used an Emoji in her texts. Rather, it was hearts, a pair lips, or a smiley face, she showed her emotions through them. I couldn't entertain her, however, I was on a high from Carter. The day was going by great and I had received several texts from Carter saying how much I meant to him and how much he loved me. I believed him. This was a different side of him. He was all in his emotions and truly showing his feelings. He was a jelly bean. Hard on the outside but soft on the inside. Only those that he loved saw that side of him. We were texting on and off until I went to lunch. I asked him if he wanted me to bring him something, but he never responded. Insecurities tried to push me in his direction, but I was always told if you go looking for trouble you'll find it. I ate lunch and continued my day. I did notice that Carter never responded, but I tried to maintain and stay positive. He had damaged my trust, but I knew that if I gave it my all,

starting from a clean slate, things would work out better. After
work I picked up the boys and headed home to prepare
dinner. As soon as I entered the house the phone was ringing.
I rushed to answer anticipating it might be Carter, but when I
answered, the caller hung up. I unpacked and got
comfortable. The phone began to ring again. As soon as I
answered, the caller hung up again. I looked at the caller I.D.
and noticed it was an unknown caller, not just this time, butt
the first time that I answered. I knew it had to be that bitch
and that's probably why Carter didn't answer my calls. He was
probably with her. I felt so angry and stupid. How could he
again? I picked up my cell and called him, no answer. I dialed
again, no answer. I tried not to break down in front the boys,
but Carter was really pissing me off. I turned off the stove and
ran in the bathroom to cry. Sitting on the floor bawling, I
continued to call him to no avail. "Mom, mom. Some woman
is knocking at the door, I heard my son yell through the
bathroom door." I nearly fell as quickly as I jumped up. My
heart sunk as I walked through the door. First Carter ignores
all of my calls, then these mysterious calls and now some
woman is knocking at my door. I trusted him again. God says
that He won't put any more on us than we could bear, so why
do I keep going through this? I slung open the door and sure
enough, it was a woman, but not the home wrecker. "And
who the fuck are you, I snapped." "I'm sorry ma'am. Are you
Sharon Camon?" My tone changed as this woman clearly
couldn't have been a mistress of Carter's. "Yes, I am. And you
are?" "I'm Sicely. Your husband said that you would be home
by now because he called and he wanted me to bring you these
beautiful roses, this card and some chocolates. I hope I didn't
disturb you. He said this is usually the time that you're cooking
and relaxed." I stood in the doorway in awe and embarrassed
at the same time. I came further out on the porch so that I
could see the car the deliverer was driving. 1-800 Pro Flowers
spanned across the driver door. "Please forgive me. I'm

beyond embarrassed." "It's quite alright. I pray that the rest of your day goes well." I watched as the woman slowly drove away. Carter has been planning this all day. He's maturing into the husband that I knew he could be.

CHAPTER 21
MIA

What in the hell is going on here? Chase and Blake are teaming up to bust me, really. I snatched my hand away from Chase. "So this is how y'all play. What's this?" "Sweetheart, what are you talking about? I want you to meet my new business partner. Why are you so upset?" I looked at Chase and he was looking like babe he doesn't know and I'm as surprised as you are. "Oh baby you know I like to have you all to myself. I wasn't expecting a guest. My apologies, sir, I said as I extended my hand back to Chase." "No problem. I won't trouble y'all lovebirds long, Chase said, smiling." After about an hour of chatting, I learned that Chase and Blake met one night at a bar and exchanged business cards. Shortly after they closed the deal and Chase was now a partner in Blake's company and also the new Operating Manager for the site here in Tampa. My husband and the man that tore us apart were

now entwined in more ways than Blake knew. Just as Chase
promised he didn't stay long. He called a cab and left. Blake
and I continued drinking and enjoying each other's company
and to my surprise, I wasn't as shaken as I was when I first sat
down. This was kind of exciting. My phone vibrated so loud
the table shook. I glanced down at my phone and noticed a
text from Chase. "Wow. Texts this late mean one or two
things, a girlfriend with a crisis or a nigga with a hard on." "It's
neither Blake. Well, if you call Kelis bitching about me
canceling on her today a crisis, then yeah you would be right, I
said laughing and showing him the text that Kelis actually sent
me earlier." I hated lying to Blake but the biggest lie was that I
already knew Chase and didn't tell him right on the spot. I
didn't get to read Chase's text in its entirety, but I did see the
words "PLAYING WITH FIRE, in all caps." Blake started
staring at me with his "I want you now" eyes. The restaurant
was looking scarce and Blake and I was still there. "Hey, baby
maybe we should get out of here, I said, grabbing Blake's
cheek." Yeah. We are about the last ones here. I'll get the tab
and the car." "Okay, baby, well, I'm about to do a last minute
lady's run and I'll be right out." I decided to go in the
bathroom and read Chase's text before we left because if I
needed to respond, I wouldn't be able to tonight. I ran into
the stall and pulled my phone out. Before I could get to Chase
text someone knocked on the stall. "Sorry. Someone is in
here, I yelled angrily." Shit, I know whoever it was could see
that. I began to read the text and someone knocked on the
door again. I slung open the door, "look." I cut my sentence
off as I saw Chase as he stood in front of the stall. "Chase,
what are you?," I couldn't even finish my sentence. Chase
grabbed my head and kissed me long and hard before he
pushed me on the sink. "Baby, wait. What if someone comes
in?" "I locked the door, baby. Let me take care of you." I
couldn't do anything but lay back as Chase tongue caressed my
inner thighs. My juices were flowing like a river. Chase

grabbed me up off the sink and bent me over the counter. I heard his pants drop and I turned around just in time to see his Man at full attention. He grabbed my hair and began to thrust my insides. Pulling my hair with each pump. This man felt so good and I quickly remembered why he had me so gone. I was in a trance and totally forgot about Blake and the mere fact that he was in the restaurant. "Baby you feel so good. I can't believe how I've been treating you. I love you baby, Chase said as he kept hitting me from behind." I felt him about to explode. He pulled out, turned me around and pushed me down just in time for his watermelon splash to quench my thirst. "Oh baby. I can't believe I'm seeing you tonight and I know that this is a shock to you, but I had no idea that this man was your husband. I saw the last name on the card, but never put two and two together." Chase talked breathlessly as he hurried to get dressed. I fixed myself and listened as he spoke. The spontaneous sex was amazing, however I was upset with him. Chase had been taking me through hell. Dissing me every time he got back with that fraction of a man. "Babe, will you say something?" "Well Chase I'm not thrilled with you working with my husband and I want you to quit." Chase looked at me in disbelief. "What. Why?" "Why. Because he's my husband and if he ever found out who you were he would probably kill your ass." "Oh he's your husband now, huh? What was he just a minute ago when I was fucking your brains out?" "Funny. Look either you quit or I will tell him who you are. I don't play games like this. I would never allow someone to pretend in my husband's face. At first this seemed exciting, but this is very dangerous Chase." I grabbed my clutch and headed for the door. As soon as I walked out, I saw Blake coming to the back. " Hey babe. I thought that you got kidnapped or something." "Oh no babe. I was just pulling myself together. It has been a long time since we have had a good time together and to be honest, I'm a little nervous. I don't know where we are headed with this and I don't want to hurt you again." Blake grabbed me by the waist and pulled my chin up to look him directly in the eyes. "Baby, enjoy the ride. Let's not talk about the past. Let's work on building our future." I sighed and walked away with my husband and tried to dismiss my sexapade.

CHAPTER 22
PARIS

After investigating, well after talking to Bryan's sister, whom I remained close to, I found out that "She," that Bryan mentioned in the text, was a girl name Amy. She lived in my city and worked at the Blockbuster movie store that Bryan and I always went to. After weeks of knowing this information and constant thinking, I also remembered seeing this woman's name in Bryan's phone one day when I was snooping. I was deeply hurt and cried almost every day. I knew this pain quite well and the only way that I could get over it was revenge. One late night I decided to call Bryan. "Hello." "So, this is how you want to play? I gave you my all Bryan and I know that you been seeing this girl for a while now." "Paris, I met her one day and we exchanged numbers but I never got up with her until we split up. I wanted things to work out between us, but

I just didn't trust the club wristband or the excuse that you gave me. When you decided to take a break, I felt like that would be best for us. Amy was just there to comfort me and things evolved. I'm sorry Paris." Bryan made sense, however, based off of what his sister said, he started seeing this girl in December and she spent New Year's with him as well. I believed her about New Years because that's when Bryan had so many excuses about his phone and the events surrounding his distance, but Bryan had his way of making me believe him even when I knew that he was lying. The more and more he spoke on this call the more upset I got and nothing made me more upset than to hear a woman laughing in the background. I couldn't believe that Bryan had this girl listening to me cry and she had the audacity to laugh at me. I slammed the phone down and rage formed deep down. I was angry and for the first time, I actually felt like I could kill someone. I didn't even have rage like this with my ex husband and he actually tried to kill me more than once. Recalling those events created more rage. I was actually able to take the gun out of William's hand the day that he kidnapped the boys and me and then I ran up the street. The closer William got to me, however, more afraid of him I got. All kinds of thoughts ran through my mind. I thought that maybe I would drop the gun or that I would miss my one opportunity and he would grab the gun and shoot me so I just threw it in the woods by the highway that we were on. I think I was more afraid to kill someone. I would have to live with that for the rest of my life and that alone would have been devastating to me. If I would have killed him, though in self defense, however, maybe I could have prevented the worst thing imagined from that entire situation. I was still devastated by the murder of my ex husband. It haunted me every day. When I met Bryan I told him about it and he expressed deep sympathy for my situation so I never imagined that he would try to hurt me just as bad. He promised me that he would never hurt me. The entire time that I sat in my bedroom that night I contemplated killing Bryan and continued to remember all of the events surrounding my marriage. Before moving to Atlanta, I found out that William had got a gun from a church member, well former church member who was also the same woman that I accused William of having a fling with. He always denied it, but when the officer told me who the gun was registered to, I knew getting out of that town was the best thing for me and my boys. I would've never suspected that someone that I knew would try to help William in his attempt to kill me. I've always heard of the cliché saying "Be careful of the grave that you dig for someone else, for it just might be the grave that you're digging for yourself." I cried and cried and didn't take that cliché saying as anything but words right now in my own situation. It was almost 1am. I packed up my boys and headed to Florida determined to hurt Bryan as bad as he had hurt me. I drove for almost 2 1/2 hours, when I happened to look in the back seat at my boys. They had been through so much and here I was about to take them through much more because of a man that I chose to get involved with. My oldest was the only one awake. He saw me crying and reached up to touch me on the shoulder, whispering, "Mom don't cry. God said that we will be okay." My son was paralyzed and had more joy in his life than I ever seemed to have. His spirit had always gotten me through rough times, but in that moment I knew that God spoke through my son to prevent me from making one of the biggest mistakes that I could ever make. God has a way of speaking to us quietly but we must be still in order to hear Him. Most situations, whether job decisions, relationship choices or making a big purchase, God speaks to us in an attempt to keep us from the turmoil and disaster. I realized that He wants the best for us and when we don't listen, we go through the worst just to get back to where He desired us to be debt free, and happy. At that moment I was listening and I was determined to be happy. Bryan may have taken advantage of my heart and of the person that I was, but it would have never happened if I would have just listened to that small Voice that told me from the beginning that this was not the man for me. I whispered to my son "thank you and I love you," and I got off of the next exit to turn around. My boys had school the next morning and even though I didn't get any sleep, I was blessed to know that the best was yet to come.

CHAPTER 23
PARIS

It had been three months since that awful night of thoughts of killing Bryan. We spoke on one or two occasions, but nothing major came from it. He was miserably happy and I was content with no longer being with him. We both cheated and both lied about it and we both had moved on. The weirdest thing that happened during our split, however, was the relationship that I formed with his baby mama. I always had a good effect on children and Bryan's daughter and I had formed an unbreakable bond. Through our continued relationship, despite her father and I breaking up, a relationship with her mother formed. Bryan had always painted Summer that was Harmony's mother, as a troublemaker who would do anything to break up his relationship and keep him away from his daughter, but why wouldn't he lie? My boy's dad was exactly the same way. Every woman that he met he painted me to be this villain that kept him away from his kids because I wanted him and he didn't want me. Exactly the opposite and I found out from Summer that that was the same case with Bryan. Nonetheless Summer and I became great friends. She told me about all the times that Bryan would come to see her in my car and how he would beg her for sex. She also told me about the hard decision that she had to endure by having an abortion or not. I was eternally grateful that she made the right decision and I know that she was too because Harmony was a doll. Bryan was such a manipulator and a liar. Summer started coming to Atlanta and anytime that I was in her town we kicked it. Summer was so beautiful. She stood about 5"2, 110 pounds. She was a model so she always watched her weight. She had these big dreamy eyes and could dress her ass off. I couldn't understand why Bryan cheated on her, she was gorgeous and had the biggest heart. We were alike in that area so I guessed that's why we clicked so well. Since my relationship was over I was single and ready to mingle. Summer was single as well, so we partied almost every weekend along with another home girl of mine, Kylah. We were three peas in a pod and we all had something in common, we all were tied to the Jungle Family Connection. Kylah was in a relationship with Bryan's brother who was doing prison time. Every now and then we allowed Bryan's sister to kick it with us also. Partying was my way of forgetting Bryan by replacing him with some random. I never got too involved, however, because industry niggas typically wanted one thing and a commitment wasn't part of the deal. To elaborate, industry niggas consisted of rappers, DJs, or producers of the music world. I had my share and tried not to get caught up in all the bullshit that they had to offer. I began to invest quality time and money into these clubs and eventually drugs. I wasn't shy to smoking weed, however Kylah smoked for breakfast, lunch and dinner so I became a social smoker whenever I chilled with her. We smoked and partied with the best of the best. Every party, we had an invite, either Summer, Kylah or I had some connection with whomever was throwing the party. All was well until I got involved with a new artist out of New York but resided in Atlanta. "Paris are you sure about this one? He seems to be a little out of your league." "Summer, I'm just having fun. What harm could he do me?" "Alright girl, just be careful." Summer was always concerned like that. She wanted the best for me and usually when she felt someone was wrong for me, she never held it back. I always kept her interests in my mind. She was the one to help me get over my hurt behind Bryan. I was amazed one night I called her crying and she prayed and uplifted me like a friend would do. This was the best thing that could've ever formed from my misfortune. That's just how God works. You never know why you meet certain people or why they are in your life. I strongly believe that I met Bryan in order to build the friendship between Summer and I. Every time that I got with ole dude, I thought about Summer's advice. He was totally out of my league. He had me doing things that I never wanted to do, but I complied simply because it kept me in the limelight. My life was spinning in another dimension. Whenever I finished dealing with one man, I moved on to the next. This particular engagement didn't last long at all. I quickly realized that Summer was right all along and this guy only wanted me when he wanted me. We smoked and chilled and he even used the "I love you," card. I was a sucker for "I love you's, but at the end of the day, that's all I was to him no matter how he tried to act differently. To get vengeance, though, I smashed his homie. He began to blast me on all social sites, especially Twitter after he found out. I never knew why I allowed men to break me down to their level because in the end, I'm left embarrassed and feeling foolish.

One day while riding, I heard an ad about an organization,

"Heel My Heart," that was having a 3-day seminar. Later that day I looked up the organization and found out that it was a non-profit Foundation that empowers women affected by domestic violence and abuse. I was a woman scorned by so many men with the first one being my own father. I needed a change and a new direction for my life to go so I was determined to start with this program.

Meanwhile, Mia and Sharon was battling the same thing. Happy one moment and devastated the next. Little did we all know that God was about to move miraculously in all of our lives. "He Ain't Dead Yet," meant something different to me than the other two ladies. For Sharon and Mia, their husbands were still alive and marriage vows state, "Till Death Do Us Part." However, for me, "He Ain't Dead Yet," simply meant that Domestic Abuse and Violence still existed in my world and the type of abusive men that I encountered were still somehow resurfacing in my life. "Sometimes the universe will give you unpleasant, disappointing, and painful experiences, but through those situations you will be guided back to the right path."

TO BE CONTINUED

EXCERPT
HOLY MATRIMONY: PARIS PREVAILS

"Paris, pass me the blunt. It's puff, puff, pass nicca," Bryan
said, coughing and laughing at the same time. "Look baby,
how much longer before this guy gets here." "Chill out. He
will be here soon." Bryan and I had been back together for a
couple of months now. I went from rappers to drug dealers to
UFC fighters to niggas with too many damn kids. During our
breakup, my partying with Summer and the gang and my
jumping in and out of men's beds and doing every drug
imaginable, landed me in the hospital. One night I went
numb. I couldn't stand, shit I could barely talk. I called my
mom and she immediately called an ambulance to come pick
me up. When they arrived, I was dehydrated and barely lucid.
My uncle and his wife came to sit with the boys and I was
carried off. Since Bryan and I had been talking, I decided to
give him a call and to my surprise, as soon as he got off he

came to my rescue. I did love my dread head rasta and I can't front, he had the best sex ever and I missed it. From that night on, Bryan and I was going strong. I hated the fact that as soon as we started kicking it again, Bryan stopped going to work. I enjoyed our time, but I hated a broke ass man. Since he worked in Florida during the week and only spent weekends with me, well early Saturday morning to late Sunday nights, he got desperate for constant attention and started calling in more than he was going. Eventually he quit and we began selling drugs together. I knew it wasn't a life that I wanted or even needed for that matter but it made Bryan happy to have money, provide for me and be with me every day. We did several runs a week because Bryan would sell out quickly. Today our plug ran late and I was getting restless and horny. I kicked my Giuseppe's up and adjusted the seat back trying to clear my mind of all the bullshit Bryan had me involved in. Nothing seemed important to me anymore, not even my health. I was 96 pounds wet and couldn't gain any weight. I spent my days running dope and my nights partying, popping and sexing Bryan down. I loved my boys, however, and I maintained just enough to be a good mother and tried not to let my lifestyle affect them. Most nights that I would pop pills I could barely get up the next morning to get them ready for school, but I did and as soon as I got them off, I slept until they were pulling up in the afternoons. A part of me hated this life, but something about it excited me. Maybe it was the money, the threesomes or maybe I was just coked out of my head to realize that I deserved better, no matter the reason, I was down to ride for my nicca.

ABOUT THE AUTHOR

Author R. Nikki Chaney continues to give her testimony. She is currently running a successful non-profit foundation, Heel My Heart, Corporation, which is based out of Atlanta, Georgia. She was inspired to establish this non-profit after publishing "Till Death Do Him Part." This foundation encourages, empowers and educates women affected by domestic violence and abuse. She continuously raise awareness to this epidemic through her novels, her foundation and Heels 4A Cause Fashion Show. Continue to support her throughout her journey.

www.ingramcontent.com/pod-product-compliance
Lightning Source LLC
Chambersburg PA
CBHW050412030726
47503CB00006B/2162